What is the Connection?

Terry Rajan

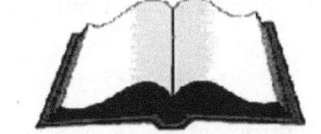

CCB Publishing
British Columbia, Canada

What is the Connection?

Copyright ©2008 by Terry Rajan
ISBN-13   978-0-9810246-0-8
First Edition

Library and Archives Canada Cataloguing in Publication

Rajan, Terry
What is the Connection? / written by Terry Rajan.
ISBN 978-0-9810246-0-8
I. Title.
PS8635.A455W53 2008   C813'.6   C2008-903827-4

United States Copyright Office Registration # TXu 984-5532
Cover design by Matt Avery.

Publisher: CCB Publishing
             British Columbia, Canada
             www.ccbpublishing.com

Chapter 1

Enumclaw, Washington
Friday, May 16, 2008
10:00 PM

Claire stood a on her house patio wearing a beautiful dress matching her golden brown long hair watching her friends one by one driving in for her sixteenth birthday. Her big blue eyes sparkling with joy and her small round face glowing. She breathed in the cool night air, smelling the fresh, clean spring scent of the farmlands. Her parents had thrown her a surprise party, inviting all of her friends from school; lots of presents and fun, it was her best birthday ever. Her friends are about to leave Claire turning back toward the house, she paused, noticing her parents standing in the living room, whispering. I wonder what's going on, she thought, as she went inside.

"Come in here, Honey bring your friends inside you have one more present to open." Another one? she thought. As she walked into the living room with her friends she saw the big box on the floor. Too excited to notice the air holes, she dropped to the floor next to the gift and excitedly ripped off the paper, flinging shreds all about her. The box started to shake and out popped the cutest puppy she had ever seen! Startled, she jumped back, and lost her balance, hitting her head against the wall, then slumping to the floor in a motionless heap. All her friends looking with shock.

"Oh my!" shouted her mother, Sandra. "Is she alright?" Carl, Claire's father, gently shook Claire's shoulder; there was no response.

"Call an ambulance, now!" he said, turning to Sandra. Sandra rushed to the phone and dialed the emergency number.

"She's not moving!" Carl heard her scream into the phone. He took the phone from Sandra and gave the operator their information. Sandra knelt by Claire, crying, talking to her, brushing the long, golden brown hair from her face, praying for her to wake up. Carl, on the line with the operator, came to sit with Claire and Sandra, putting his arms around Sandra to calm her. It seemed like it took forever for the ambulance to arrive, even though it was only a matter of minutes. The medics arrived and checked Claire's vital signs, verified that she appeared to still be unconscious, then loaded her into the ambulance and rushed her to the hospital; her parents followed in their car. Sandra and Carl were directed to the waiting room for the doctor to update them on Claire's condition. They sat together, fearing the worst, would she gain consciousness, would she be alright? They were so distracted with their thoughts they didn't notice the doctor approaching.

"Sandra, Carl?" their family physician, Dr. James Cannon said as he approached them; fortunately, he was on call that night. "Claire is awake, and appears to be fine, she just has a bump on the head. We did CAT scan and didn't find any damage, but we would like to keep her overnight for observation. I don't see any reason why she can't go home in the morning." Sandra and Carl were visibly relieved. Dr. Cannon showed them Claire's room so they could see for themselves she was recovered.

When Claire woke up the next morning, she couldn't figure out where she was until she remembered what had happened with the puppy. The head nurse noticed her disorientation and called for Dr. Cannon.

"Good morning, Claire. How are you feeling today?" Dr. Cannon checked her vital signs. She looked up at him with a puzzled frown.

"I'm not sure" she said very quietly.

"Are you in pain?" Dr. Cannon asked as he pulled up a chair

next to Claire's bed. Claire hesitated. Well, no, it's not that. I just...oh, you wouldn't believe me if I told you." Dr. Cannon patted her hand in a fatherly manner.

"Well, I've known you all your life, I would certainly try to believe anything you tell me, you've always been very honest". Claire looked up at him with her big blue eyes, brimming with tears.

"When I hit my head, I don't think I was really knocked unconscious. I could see things, but they weren't things in my living room. I felt as though someone had pushed me, and I was lying on a thickly carpeted floor. I get the sense it was a bedroom and it was mine, but it didn't look anything like my bedroom at home. Across the room, I could see someone taking money and boxes out of a big safe. I actually felt like I was someone else." Claire hung her head, letting her tears slip down her cheeks. "I know it sounds crazy..."

"Now, Claire, don't be so hard on yourself," Dr. Cannon smiled. "It doesn't sound crazy at all. Head injuries are traumatic and the mind does strange things to distract you from pain. I'm sure you'll be your own cheerful self in a day or two. I'll call your parents and let them know they can take you home." He didn't tell her parents what Claire said, merely cautioned them against letting her "overdo" for the next couple of days.

Chapter 2

The next morning, Carl and Sandra agreed that Claire should stay home from school, and let her sleep as long as she needed. When she awoke, she came down into the kitchen, where Sandra was cleaning.

"Mother," she said, "I need to talk to Dr. Cannon again." Sandra took one look at her face and dropped her rag in the sink.

"What is it, Dear?" she asked, concerned. "Does your head really hurt?"

"No, but...I think I need to tell him more of my memories, I think we better go and see the doctor."

"Okay, dear, I'll call him." When she got the doctor on the phone, and repeated what Claire had told her, he confided that she had mentioned something to him about being disoriented during her unconsciousness.

"I've been thinking," he said, "that maybe she should see a colleague of mine, Dr. Jane Radcliff. She deals with brain injury and shock disorder. I'll see if I can get you an appointment and call you back."

"Thank you, Dr. Cannon." Sandra hung up and told Claire what the doctor had said. Claire went upstairs to get dressed in case he was able to get her an appointment right away. When Claire came back into the kitchen, her mother told her that Dr. Radcliff was expecting them as soon as they could get to Seattle. "I called your father and told him we were going into the city. Are you ready to go?"

"I am a little nervous but I should be okay, Mum." The drive to Seattle was made in silence. Claire stared out the window, admiring the beautiful Washington scenery. In early spring, the flowers were beginning to bloom, and the trees were just starting to unfold their leaves, hinting at the promise of new life. Sandra was preoccupied with trying to navigate the narrow country roads.

Arriving at the doctor's office, they introduced themselves to the receptionist and mentioned that Dr. Cannon had called to schedule the appointment. She immediately buzzed Dr. Radcliff, letting her know of their arrival. Across the room a door opened, and a woman of about thirty-five years, with rich chestnut-colored, shoulder-length hair, striking green eyes, and a slight build, approached them.

"Claire Warner?" she asked, smiling warmly. Claire nodded and stepped forward to shake her hand. "It's nice to meet you, Claire, and this is your mother, Sandra?" Sandra also nodded and shook hands. "Dr. Cannon didn't tell me the whole story of why he was sending you here; it's better if I hear it from you, anyway. But first, let's do some preliminary testing." She led the way into a small room with a table and chair. On the table were papers and a pencil. "Have a seat, Claire. I have some questions that I would like you to answer. Don't think too hard about them; just write down what comes to mind. Okay? The last page is some simple math just to check out your brain." She winked, drawing a small smile from Claire. "Meanwhile, I would like to talk with your mother." Claire seemed to visibly relax, settled into the chair and began the test. Dr. Radcliff left the room, but didn't close the door. She motioned Sandra to a seating area that was positioned so that Claire could still see them, but where they were out of earshot.

"Now, suppose you give me a brief rundown of why you think Claire needs to be here." Sandra took a deep breath. "Well, Saturday was Claire's birthday, and we surprised her with a puppy. When it leaped out of the box at her, she ducked sideways and hit her head against the wall. Dr. Cannon checked her out, he even kept her until the next morning; everything seemed fine. Now she says she feels funny, but her head doesn't hurt – just a funny feeling, like an out of body experience. I'm worried about her." At this point, Sandra's voice broke, and she fumbled in her purse for a tissue.

"I must ask just a few more questions, if you don't mind," Dr. Radcliff said sympathetically. "Does Claire have any drinking or drug problems?"

"No, she never drinks and she only has a few friends, but they are all from good families; we know all of them. She is the best teenager you could wish for."

"Has she had any mental or other unusual behavior in the past?"

"Like I said before, Claire is the best, she has never behaved abnormally."

"OK, I'll take your word on that." Dr. Radcliff glanced into the room where Claire was, but Claire was concentrating on the papers. "Why don't you just sit here and relax while Claire and I discuss this in my office," she suggested. "Young people tend to talk more freely without their parents' presence."

As Dr. Radcliff stood in the doorway, Claire looked up. "All finished?" Claire nodded and stood up, handing her the papers. "Let's go into my office, then." Dr. Radcliff led Claire into her office, and had her take a seat in an easy chair. Taking a notebook from her desk, she sat in the opposite chair and briefly looked through what Claire had written.

"Well, the math problems are all correct, and I don't see anything abnormal about any of your other answers." She looked up and smiled. "I can pretty much rule out any physical damage. Have you had any trouble walking, dizzy spells, bumping into things?"

"No," said Claire. "Physically, I feel fine. My head doesn't even hurt any more."

"So, in other ways you are not fine? Can you explain that to me?"

"It sounds so crazy, I'm sure people are going to laugh at me. This kind of stuff only happens in the movies or something." Claire's eyes filled with tears, and Dr. Radcliff handed her a box of tissues. She then gave Claire an encouraging nod, and sat back to listen. "Well, when I hit my head on the wall" Claire began, "I fell down on the floor, only, suddenly, it wasn't my floor, it was a thick carpet in a beautiful room, and I could feel something very soft and light against my skin, like I was wearing a silky nightgown. Across the room, someone was pulling money and boxes out of a safe, and I knew it was my safe, but there was nothing I could do. I knew the person had pushed me and I had hit my head, I felt like I was dying." Claire blew her nose, and then continued. "Ever since, I keep remembering more and more about 'myself'. I lived in New York City. I was very rich and lived in a big house with servants – or at least a housekeeper," she frowned, "that part's not really clear. I remember that my father was a very tall and powerful man, and my mother was dead. We had a lot of trees around our house and a beautiful garden in the back."

"We? You lived with your father?" Dr. Radcliff asked.

"No, I was married...I think." Again, she frowned, trying to bring the memory into focus. "No, Claire, don't force it. The memories, if that's what they are, have to come on their own."

"You don't believe me?" Fresh tears flowed now, and Claire made a move as if to get up out of the chair.

"It's not that I don't believe you, it's just that I don't want to influence any thoughts or feelings you might have. Now, you said the person had pushed you, and that is when you hit your head?"

"Yes, on the wall, no wait, the mantle! That's it, we had a marble fireplace in the bedroom, and I hit my head on it as I fell!"

"Alright, I think that's enough for now. I think it would be helpful to keep a journal of what comes to mind about this, then we will get together and see what we can do about clearing it out of your mind."

"I forgot to tell you something that might be important; I think my name is or was, Christina. Christina Solderburg Kingsbury." Claire stated flatly. At this, Claire seemed to lose all her energy and slumped back in the chair. Dr. Radcliff got up and put her notes on her desk. Leaving Claire alone in her office, she approached Sandra in the waiting area.

"Claire has had an exhausting day, I think she should go home and get some rest. Try to not let her talk about this too much. I've asked her to keep a journal of what she feels. If she wants to discuss it with you, that's fine, but have her write everything down." They had been walking toward Dr. Radcliff's office and now drew Claire into the conversation. "I suggest that you don't mention this to anyone at school, either. Young people are prone to sensationalize things, and I don't want them making up memories and feelings for you." Claire nodded as she picked up her things, and allowed her mother to lead her from the room.

After they left, Dr. Radcliff sat down and organized her notes. A very interesting case, she thought. Definitely something worth looking into. Before leaving for lunch, Jane asked her secretary to check the Internet on Christina Solderburg and the Warner family in the local Enumclaw newspaper.

All through lunch, Jane played Claire's words over and over in her mind. She had purposely left her notes on her desk, but that did no good. She couldn't leave the story alone; it demanded her full attention. Since she had no appointments for the rest of the day, she grabbed her notes, and headed for the library in downtown Seattle. The librarian set her up with the microfilm machine, leaving Jane alone to begin her search, looking through back issues of The New York Times. Surely, if Christina and her father were as rich and powerful as Claire said, her murder would have been headline news. Jane began by looking back five years, then ten, and fifteen. Jane was about to give up when suddenly a headline caught her eye.

"New York Times, December 23rd, 1992: Mike Kingsbury has been sentenced to life in prison for his wife's murder" The trial had lasted for five months, the story said. Jane printed it out, then went back to the Monday of that week. She found nothing about the trial for the previous week. Confused, she re-read the story she had printed. There! The trial had started on the 22nd of July, 1992. Excited now, she found the paper for the 23rd of July, 1992, and began to print every word about the trial. Skimming through the lines, she noted the date of the murder, May 16th, 1992. Once she had the information on the trial printed out, she went back to the May 17th, 1992 papers, and printed out everything she could find on the murder and the investigation, right up to the arrest of the husband. It didn't seem to take very long to focus on him, she thought, but then, the spouse is always suspected. She turned in the films to the librarian, and took her printouts to a table to study. Socialite Christina Kingsbury was found dead in her bedroom by her housekeeper, the paper reported. She had bled to death from a head wound, and had been robbed of everything in her bedroom safe. This happened sixteen years ago, how could Claire know anything about this? Jane thought to herself. She gathered her papers up and, upon arriving at her office, Jane checked with her secretary to see if she found anything on the Internet.

"I found an article that mentions Christina Kingsbury's murder in 1992. I also called the Enumclaw Courier-Herald to see what they have on the Warners, they said they couldn't find anything, but, the lady I talked to knows them personally and said that they are a good family. When the lady asked who I was, I said I was with a Seattle school and was wondering about Claire's character; she seemed satisfied with my answer."

"OK, well, thanks for looking."

Looking up the Warner number, she called, hoping one of Claire's parents would answer. Sandra picked up the phone on the third ring, sounding a little out of breath. "Sandra? It's Dr. Jane Radcliff. I have a few questions for you concerning Claire. I hope I'm not disturbing you?"

"No, I was just out back. How can I help you?"

"How old did Claire turn on her birthday Wednesday and has she ever been to New York?"

"It was her sixteenth birthday, and no, she's never been out of Washington State, except the time we went skiing in Idaho when she was eight. Is something wrong?" Sandra asked, becoming concerned.

"No, but, I may have some very interesting news for all of you. Would it be too inconvenient if I came out there?"

"All the way to Enumclaw? This must be important! Certainly you may come. In fact, I will insist that you stay for dinner."

"That would be very nice. I'll come out now, I'd like to talk to Claire as soon as possible."

When Jane arrived at the Warner home, Claire answered the door.

"Hello, Dr. Radcliff, won't you come in? Mother said you wanted to talk to me; we can sit in the living room while my folks fix dinner." She led the way into the room, motioning for the doctor to sit on the sofa.

"Claire, I went to the library today, to see if I could substantiate your story. I wanted to see if what you have are truly memories. Now, before I go any further, I have a couple of questions and I want you to give me completely honest answers." Claire seemed a little nervous at this, but she nodded. "Have you been doing any research for school that involves reading The New York Times?"

"No, we do most of our research for school from the Seattle Times or the Enumclaw Courier-Herald if we need a newspaper."

"How far back do you usually have to go?"

"Well, last year, one teacher had us look up sports records back to the opening of the school, but, usually it's current events, within the past month or so. Why?"

"When I went to the library, I looked through the microfilms of The New York Times to see if I could find the names you mentioned. Did you remember anything else? Have you written it down?" Claire was silent. Then she began to speak in a soft, hollow voice, as if she were speaking to no one in particular.

"I remembered that I was definitely married. My husband was handsome, but my father didn't like him." Jane reached over and took Claire's hand.

"I don't want to upset you, Claire, but I found the names. Two days before you were born, a Christina Kingsbury was found dead in her bedroom. She'd been robbed, and died of a blow to the head. A few days later, her husband was arrested for the crime. He was tried and sentenced to life in prison just six months after his wife was killed."

"No! Mike would never...I mean, we argued, but...he wouldn't kill me, would he?" This last was said directly to Dr. Radcliff, almost as a plea. Just for a moment, she almost felt that there was someone else asking the question. Then, something Claire had said sunk in.

"Whom did you say?"

"Mike, my husband." Claire said automatically. She then froze. "How did I know that? You didn't mention his name!" Claire exclaimed.

"No, I didn't." Jane said gently. "Let's focus for now on your life instead of your death, shall we? Can you remember what your house looked like?" Closing her eyes, Claire nodded. "Let's get some paper and see how closely you can draw it. I'll also want a rough map of the surrounding area, and some details." Claire went into the adjoining office and gathered a pencil and some paper for drawing. As she sat down and began drawing, Jane continued with her questions.

"What did Mike do for a living, do you remember?"

"Yes, he was a designer. No, that's not right", Claire's brow creased, "architect, that's it. He had his own company. They designed and built new buildings, pools..." her voice trailed off, a look of pain passed over her face, and the moment was over. Claire finished her drawing and turned it so that Dr. Radcliff could see it.

"Here, that's the house; the front of it as you drive up. If you see it from the air like we do in Daddy's helicopter, it looks like this." She drew a sketch of the house and grounds. "This is my garden," she smiled wistfully. "I love my garden." Then she drew the house smaller, and added the streets around it, pointing out houses she had been in, and the nearby park. "That's all I remember."

"Well, I'd say that's quite enough for now," Jane was astonished at the clarity with which the memories were coming now. It was almost as if... before she could finish that thought, Sandra appeared in the doorway and announced that dinner was ready. Jane placed the sketches in her briefcase and followed Claire and Sandra to the dining room. Carl was home, and over dinner, Jane asked Carl and Sandra to tell her how they met, married, about Claire's birth, her childhood. Jane wondered if there was anything in Carl or Sandra's past that might give a clue as to Claire's mental history. A smile broke out on Sandra's face and her eyes showed a hint of a twinkle as her mind drifted back to when she and Carl met.

Chapter 3

They had both been at the Post Office and had literally run into each other. After laughingly untangling her purse strap from his tool belt, they introduced themselves. She commented, trying to sound casual, that their parents were friends, and she would probably see him around. The very next day, as if directed by Fate, he had walked into the bank where she worked to open an account. Sandra couldn't help but stare openly at him as he talked to the woman in New Accounts, his brown eyes flashing flirtatiously in her direction. Once, he looked up and caught her watching him, and with a wink and smile managed to embarrass her so thoroughly that she had trouble with the next several transactions. About the time she recovered her equilibrium, she looked up straight into his eyes.

"We meet again," he said softly

"Yes," she managed to say, breathlessly, ducking her head; she hid behind her long blond hair as she busied herself with his deposit. By the time he left, they had a date for dinner. From then on, they were rarely seen apart. She enjoyed introducing him once again to his charming small hometown and all the changes that had taken place since he'd been away at college and in the military. Seeing everything through his eyes, she marveled at the beauty of the place, appreciating it like she hadn't since she was a child. With Carl she found renewed joy on beautiful Mt. Rainier looming over the quaint houses and streets. The rolling pasture just past town seemed greener and the Lupine blooming in the foothills seemed miraculous in various shades of purple and pink.

One Sunday morning, the doorbell pealed loudly in the small-town early-morning silence. Sandra automatically glanced at her clock and frowned. "Who in their right mind visits anyone at eight o'clock on a Sunday morning?"

"Sandra," her father called from the master bedroom, "can you get that?"

"Sure Dad," she answered cheerfully, "I'm already dressed." Running lightly down the stairs, she peeked out the window in the front door.

"Carl!" she exclaimed with delight, flinging open the front door. "What are you doing here this early? Please don't tell me you have to work today, of all days, and are going to miss the church picnic?" she asked.

"No," said Carl seriously. "It's not that. Could I talk to you out on the porch for a minute?" Immediately Sandra sobered, opening the screen door and joining Carl on the porch.

"Is something wrong with your parents?" she inquired softly, concern clouding her soft brown eyes. Carl didn't answer; he simply took her hand and led her to a wicker chair. Seating her gently, he then moved around in front of her. As he took a small red velvet box out of his pocket, he knelt down on one knee.

"Sandra, will you marry me?"

Sandra's mouth flew open but no words came out. She was stunned. Her mind was reeling with the idea of marriage. They hadn't even discussed it!

"Sandra, are you alright?" his blue eyes searched her face for a hint of what she might say.

She shook her head as if clearing the cobwebs of doubt.

"Of course, I'm alright. You just surprised me, that's all. The answer is definitely yes, I will marry you!" Slipping the traditional engagement ring on her finger, Carl pulled her out of the chair, wrapped his arms around her and kissed her so tenderly that she felt as if a butterfly had lit on her lips. She looked at her hand where the engagement ring encircled her finger and felt a profound sense of joy in the symbol of their love. "Let's go tell your parents now, so we can announce it at church this morning," he said.

As they stepped inside the front door, Sandra's parents came down the stairs, questioning looks on their faces. "Carl, is something wrong?" Sandra's father asked.

"Not unless you have some objection to my marrying your daughter," Carl replied with a grin.

"Honey!" her mother exclaimed. "How wonderful!" She hugged Sandra, then Carl, then Sandra again. "I wish we had some champagne to celebrate!"

"On a Sunday morning? Wouldn't that cause some talk," her father winked at Carl as they all walked into the kitchen. Sandra and her mother were chatting happily and making plans.

"When is the happy day?" Her father asked. Sandra's parents looked questioningly from Carl to Sandra who both looked blankly at each other.

"Up to you, Honey," Carl said, already sounding like a doting husband.

"July 6th," said Sandra, "The anniversary of the day we met in the post office."

"Very romantic, but that doesn't give us much time," her mother said. "How in the world are we going to..."

"Now, Mom," Sandra broke in, "We don't want anything fancy. I'm sure between you, me and Mrs. Warner..." The doorbell interrupted Sandra's protest, almost as if on cue.

"Speaking of Mom, that must be my folks coming over to see if she said yes." Carl said, grinning.

"Well, I hope you'll all stay for breakfast. There's no time to go home now before church." Sandra's mother reached for her apron.

"That's just what I was thinking," Carl's mother added as she entered the kitchen, carrying food. "Here's our contribution, we great cooks must think alike!" The mothers shared a laugh and conspired together regarding wedding plans while cooking. Breakfast was quickly prepared, eaten, and both families set off to church.

Afterward, the congregation gathered around the couple with congratulations and the church picnic was turned into an impromptu engagement party. Sandra looked around, basking in her own joy and the happiness around her.

"There just couldn't possibly be any more wonderful place to live than this!" She thought to herself.

Chapter 4

Several months after the wedding, Sandra groaned as the bright morning sunshine streamed into the bedroom. One hour to get to work and the last thing she wanted to do was get out of bed. But she did, just in time to make it to the bathroom. If only she had kept Carl home from work! She picked up the phone on her nightstand.

"Mother? Are you busy? I need a ride to the doctor. I don't know, I think it's the flu or something. Can you come? Thanks!" She hung up, then picked up the phone again. "Doug? It's Sandra. I won't be in today. I picked up a flu bug or something. Oh, thanks. I should be alright tomorrow." Hanging up, she got dressed, stopping twice to race into the bathroom. When her mother arrived, she took one look at her face, noticing the greenish tinge, and hurried her into the car.

Doctor Malcolm offered Sandra and her mother a reassuring smile. He had known Sandra since the day she was born, and was very close to the family.

"Now then, what seems to be the problem? Sandra, you aren't feeling well?" He looked over the notes the admitting nurse had made. "Blood pressure ok, pulse a little high. How long have you been sick?" Sandra took a deep breath. Dr. Malcolm's quiet voice calmed her down, and she was able to still the panic in her voice.

"Well, I felt a little dizzy and queasy the last couple days, but I chalked it up to the heat. But this morning I was sick to my stomach. Is that heat stroke, or something more serious?"

"I'll have to run some blood tests, it could be serious." His blue eyes twinkled at her; for a moment, he almost looked like Santa

Claus. "Depending on how soon you and Carl were planning on starting a family." He put down the file and folded his hands on top of it. "Unless I miss my guess, you must have conceived right away, on your honeymoon."

"Oh my goodness!" Her mother exclaimed. "I'm going to be a grandmother!"

"Now, let's not be shouting it from the rooftops just yet, let me run the tests. I'll give you a call tomorrow. Can I call you at work?" Sandra nodded numbly. "Good, I should have the results back before lunch, or would you rather come in here?" She shook her head. Doctor Malcolm smiled, "Why don't you go on home and rest for the day. I'll talk to you tomorrow."

On the way home, Sandra was subdued.

"Honey, what's wrong," her mother asked gently, "aren't you happy about this? Or are you afraid that Carl won't be happy?"

"Oh, Mother, we haven't even discussed children, yet. I'm not sure we can afford to start a family right away." Sandra sounded dispirited.

"Well, he surprised you with the proposal, you can surprise him with the baby, and don't worry about money, you have all four grandparents here, you know we will spoil our first grandchild." Sandra smiled, but said nothing. Her mother dropped her off at home, and all Sandra could think about was going in to lie down and rest.

When Carl came home, he noticed she looked a little pale. "Bad day at the bank, Babe?" He put his hands on her shoulders and kneaded gently.

"Actually, I didn't go to work today, I wasn't feeling well. It's been coming on for a couple days. Dr. Malcolm took some tests. He'll tell me tomorrow if it's anything serious." Sandra was glad Carl was behind her and could not see her face color at the half-truth. She just couldn't bring herself to mention the baby until she was sure. Better to have a fight about a sure thing than a possibility. She tried to pin down why she was uneasy about Carl's reaction, but only succeeded in giving herself a headache.

After dinner, she told Carl she was going to lie down. He offered to clean up the kitchen, and told her she might as well go to bed.

"I've got some calculations to go over on this latest contract, so I'll work in the study, and try not to wake you when I come to bed." Sandra was almost in tears at his kindness. She kissed him on the cheek and left the room before he could see her distress and demand an explanation.

The next morning, Carl was up and in the kitchen when Sandra got sick, and she managed to get them both out the door and off to work without revealing her secret. All her co-workers at the bank showed concern at her wan appearance, but she assured them that she would be fine. Just as she was closing her window for lunch, her supervisor announced that she had a phone call.

"This is Sandra", she said anxiously into the receiver.

"Sandra, this is Dr. Malcolm." Sandra's heart skipped.

"What were the results?" she asked.

"Congratulations, Sandra, you are going to be a mother. Give me a call next week, and we'll set up some appointments for you."

"Are you sure?" asked Sandra. "There's no doubt?" He assured her that the tests were very accurate, and asked if she was alright. "Yes," she lied, "I'm fine, just a little surprised." She thanked him and hung up the phone, her hand shaking ever so slightly. Her supervisor approached her, noting that she looked ill.

"Is everything alright?" he asked, looking concerned.

"Yeah, I just got the results from some tests that the doctor ran yesterday."

"Sandra, you should go home. You look like you're not over whatever you've got. We don't want the whole bank coming down with it." Sandra laughed weakly at the irony.

"No, I'm not over it, but it's not contagious. Just the same, I'll take you up on that half day off."

"Good. Do you need a ride or are you ok to drive?"

"Yes, I can drive, thank you, Doug, I can make it home."

All the way home, she rehearsed what she was going to say to

Carl. As she walked in the front door, the phone rang. "Sandra! I just called the bank and they said you went home sick. Did Dr. Malcolm call? What did he say? Were the tests positive?" Her mother sounded almost as worried as Sandra was. Sandra took a deep breath before answering.

"Calm down, Mother, before you erupt like Mt. Saint Helens! Yes, the tests were positive, I'm pregnant. What am I going to tell Carl?" Her mother sighed.

"Just tell him the truth, Honey, everything will work out just fine, you'll see. Right now, you go and put your feet up and relax. What time does Carl get home tonight?" She thought a minute.

"It's Friday, he should be home by five. Why do you ask?"

"I want you to just rest, and when he gets home, tell him right away. That way, he'll have plenty of time to react either way. I'll call his parents, and between his mother and I, we will fix dinner and bring it over around six thirty. Then you can make the official announcement. How does that sound?"

"It sounds wonderful," she said. "I wasn't looking forward to cooking tonight. Thank you so much, Mother." As she hung up the phone, Sandra took another deep breath. She decided a bubble bath would help her relax and think. She was just climbing into some fresh clothing when she heard Carl's car.

He came in the front door calling her name.

"Sandra! Honey, where are you? Are you alright?" She came downstairs and walked right into his arms.

"I was worried when I saw your car, you came home early. Are you still sick? What did the doctor say about the tests? Is it serious?" Carl pelted her with questions anxiously.

"Carl, slow down! Yes, I came home early. No, it wasn't because I got sick; I did that this morning before I left for work. Dr. Malcolm said the tests were positive." She held her breath, wondering if Carl was going to be able to read between the lines.

"Positive? Positive for what? What have you got?" His blue eyes clouded over as he considered all the possible diseases they could be facing. He looked adorable to Sandra, like a little boy, as he failed to understand the obvious.

"Oh, the doctor said I may only have about six and a half months to go." she said, leaning back to watch his face. She could feel her heart pounding in her chest. Her entire future seemed in the balance, resting on Carl's response. At first, he just looked at her quizzically, at the light in her eyes. She couldn't be talking about dying, could she? Then she saw recognition dawn in his eyes.

"A baby?" He asked incredulously. "We're going to have a baby?" Sandra nodded, then squealed as Carl picked her up and spun her around.

"Are you really happy, Carl?" Sandra was still unsure. "We hadn't talked about children yet..."

"I'm so happy, I could climb a mountain. Let's call our parents!" He set her down and reached for the phone. "Which ones first?"

"Mother knows, she took me to the doctor so she probably told Dad. Call your parents." Sandra was almost in tears again. She had a feeling this was going to be a frequent occurrence. As she listened to Carl's end of the conversation with the future grandparents, she was finally able to convince herself that everything really was going to be alright.

Over a leisurely late breakfast, Carl and Sandra enjoyed an animated discussion regarding baby names. With the baby due any day now, Sandra was starting to become worried that they had not been successful in finding a name.

"I have an idea," announced Carl. "I think we should name the baby after someone in the family."

"Well, alright, but we have parents and grandparents on both sides, not to mention numerous aunts and uncles, how do we choose?" Sandra asked skeptically. "We can't just put all the names in a hat."

"People say that girls tend to favor their fathers, and boys tend to favor their mothers, so I'll choose a girl's name from my side of the family, and you choose a boy's name from yours."

"That sounds fair." Sandra leaned back and closed her eyes to think. Carl did the same. When she opened her eyes, he was already smiling. "Well?" she asked.

"Claire," he stated firmly. "My grandmother's name was Clara, but that's a bit old fashioned, besides, Grandpa always shortened it to Claire."

"What about a middle name?" Sandra asked.

"Elizabeth for my mother," he suggested.

"Claire Elizabeth Warner," Sandra said, trying out the name. "I like it. I can't decide between William Robert and Robert William. Since Robert is my father, I'll follow your example and make it the middle name."

"Where does William come from?" asked Carl.

"My great-grandfather, he died when I was six. I always thought he was Santa Claus. He had the perfect beard for it," she grinned

"William Robert Warner. Sounds distinguished."

"Well, let's hope he..." Sandra jumped in her seat. "I'm almost sure we're having a girl. Every time I say 'he', I get kicked."

"Well, maybe he is just letting you know how much he likes his name," Carl grinned.

"As long as the baby is healthy, it doesn't matter to you if we have a girl or a boy, does it?" Sandra asked. Whenever Carl talked about the baby, he referred to 'our son'. She didn't want him to be disappointed.

"Honey," he said gently, "if we have a girl, there's a better chance the baby will look like you. What could make me happier?" He kissed her.

Life was wonderful!

Chapter 5

Enumclaw, Washington
May 16, 1992
11:38 PM

"Carl!" Sandra doubled over in pain. This was the worst one yet. "It's time to go...now!" Carl and his mother ran in from the other room.

"Are you sure, Honey?" he asked, then took a look at Sandra's face. "Never mind, of course you're sure. I'll go get the car." As he went out to the garage, the doorbell rang. It was Sandra's mother, and together the two future grandmothers got Sandra's things together for the hospital.

"It's up and running, let's go!" Carl called as he came through the door. The mothers bundled Sandra into the front seat and climbed in the back.

"Now, don't break any speed limits, but don't dawdle." Sandra's mother suggested. Smiling, Carl got behind the wheel and started for the hospital. It took all his concentration not to let go of the wheel and hold Sandra every time she had another contraction. He met her eyes, and she smiled.

"Just get me there, Honey," she said, happy even in her pain.

When they arrived at the hospital, there was a flurry of activity. Sandra had a team of nurses taking her blood pressure, setting up an I.V., and monitoring both her heart and the baby's. The strong steady sound from the monitor served as a reassurance for Carl that all was going well. He soon found himself on the sidelines. It was not long at all until the two expectant grandmothers and the father to be were in the waiting room. There they all sat quietly, literally on the edge of their seats, waiting breathlessly for the first sound from the delivery room. Finally, after what seemed an eternity, a nurse approached him, smiling. Seeing her smile, he was reassured that all had gone well.

"Mr. Warner?" He nodded, eagerly; he tried to speak to her but no words came.

"Congratulations! You are the father of a baby girl, eight pounds, six ounces. Mother and baby are doing just fine, and you can see them in about twenty minutes," she announced cheerfully.

"Thank you, God! he shouted, "and welcome to the world, Claire Elizabeth Warner! Thank you!" he said cheerfully. He bounced over to each of the new grandmothers, picked them up in his big burley arms and then spun them around, then hugged each one in turn. Carl turned the phrase over in his mind, "Mother and baby are doing just fine." Carl felt an enormous weight lifted from his shoulders, he didn't realize that he'd been so tense! He was a father, and his lovely sweet Sandra was doing well. His bliss must have shown immediately for the nurse and the new grandmothers paused in their animated conversation to look at him and smile. When the baby was brought out, Carl carefully held her and marveled at how perfect she was, from her perfect toes, to her perfect fingers. He laughed to himself thinking, what a long name for such a little girl. Carl finally became a believer in 'love at first sight'. His new daughter mesmerized him, from the instant he saw her.

"Wonderful story", Jane said, not finding anything unusual with their love, marriage or Claire's birth. Jane reminded Claire not to talk about her memories, and especially not to her school friends.

"Remember to write any new memories and feelings down in your journal. In fact, if you think they are very important, feel free to call and leave them on my office machine. I'll give you my card before I leave tonight. If you notice Claire becoming upset about this, don't hesitate to call me," she told Carl and Sandra. "Something like this can be very confusing at her age." They assured her that they would keep a close eye on Claire. Jane went to say goodnight, and found Claire in the living room with her new puppy. Claire seemed to have put all of it out of her mind, and was just being a sixteen-year-old. . Jane could hardly wait to get to the bottom of this case. She had never come across anything quite like it in her career. Besides, Claire needed to get on with the life she had, and not be burdened with someone else's. But what if...well, time would tell.

Chapter 6

Claire reached over and turned on the lamp on her nightstand. Seeing Dr. Radcliff's card poking out of her journal, she dialed the number on the card. As she waited for the answering machine to pick up, her hands were shaking and her heart was pounding. Instead of the machine picking up, she heard Dr. Radcliff's voice say, "Hello?"

"Dr. Radcliff? Oh, I didn't expect you to answer; this is Claire Warner. I remembered something very important," her heart pounding even harder. "It wasn't my husband."

"What wasn't your husband, Claire?" Dr. Radcliff sounded confused.

"The person in the bedroom, the one who pushed me. It wasn't Mike." Claire said quietly.

"Who was it?"

"I can't quite get that part. It was someone I knew very well, but I wasn't close to." Sighing, she said, "I know that doesn't make much sense, but every time I try to focus on the person's face and remember who it was, I get these shooting pains in my head."

"Ok, let it go, Claire. Don't try to remember. Just be content with what you did remember, and let the rest come by itself. Write down everything that you just told me, in case you don't remember it in the morning. Then get some sleep. I'm going to be attending a conference in New York, and when I'm there I'll look into all of this. That's why I wanted the pictures. I'll still check my messages, though, so call if anything else comes to mind."

"Alright, thank you, Doctor." Claire hung up the phone, and noted her new memories in her journal. Then she turned off the light and tried to take Dr. Radcliff's advice, but it was a long time before sleep claimed her.

In Seattle, Dr. Radcliff was also writing down what Claire had told her. What if this was real? What if an innocent man had been sent to prison and Claire had the means of freeing him? But if this was possession or channeling, why wait so long? And if it was reincarnation, as she suspected, why hadn't Claire caught glimpses of this other life before. Sighing, she gathered up her things to go home. She had a feeling sleep would not come easy until this was solved.

Jane tried to focus on what the flight attendant was saying, but she hadn't slept very well last night. She had stayed up and read every article she had printed out at the library, then decided to see if the Internet held more information on the murder trial. Sure enough, she found details from the trial that had not been printed in the paper. She printed as much information as she could find, and planned to read it on the plane; if she could stay awake, that is.

Landing in New York, she barely had enough time to get checked in before the first meeting of the convention. She looked over the schedule they were given, good, she didn't have to be at any of the morning sessions tomorrow; she could explore the area where Claire claimed to have lived. Turning her attention to the speaker at the podium, she tried to concentrate on why she was here. Tomorrow would come soon enough, and she could check out more details of Claire's story. Later, she planned to call a college friend of hers who just might know something. She hoped to go home with good news for the Warners.

"Taxi!" Jane flagged down the cab in front of her hotel. She had the three sketches Claire had done, as well as a map, and her briefcase full of printouts. Settling into the back seat, she gave the driver the address.

"Oh, the old Kingsbury place?" He pulled out into traffic as he spoke.

"It's still called that?" Jane was amazed. "But surely other people have lived there in the last sixteen years?"

"Oh, yeah, other people live there now. But it's always been called the Kingsbury place, because it was a big murder case. When a rich lady gets killed by her husband, it becomes famous. I wouldn't be surprised if they make one of those bed-and-breakfast places out of it," he said, chuckling.

"Here you are." The cab driver pulled into the curb in front of large iron gates. "You getting out, or do you just wanted to see it?"

"I'm getting out. I have some other things to look at in the area." She paid her fare and climbed out of the cab. Moving to where she could see the front of the house, she compared it to the sketch Claire had made. Yes, this was the house she 'remembered' and the other sketch clearly showed the front lawn and grounds she was looking at. Walking around the block, she looked for the places on the third sketch. One or two buildings were different, but they were also obviously new. Claire had drawn Christina's neighborhood with frightening accuracy. She returned to her hotel and had lunch, then went to her afternoon conference sessions, but she couldn't stop thinking about Claire Warner and Christina Kingsbury. Was it possible?

The next morning, Jane made a phone call. She had gone to college with a woman who later went to work in the DA's office here in New York City. Would she know about this case? Someone picked up on the third ring.

"Hello?"

"Anita? It's Jane Radcliff. How are you?"

"Jane!" Anita Templeton exclaimed, "I'm fine, and you?"

"Well, I'm in town for two reasons, one is a conference, the other is a case that I'm working on and I was hoping you could help me, are you busy? I was hoping you could you meet me for lunch."

"I would love to have lunch, where are you staying?"

She gave Anita the name of her hotel. "Do you mind coming

here? I'd come out there, but if we get to talking, I may be late getting back."

"Not at all, I can be there by one p.m., is that okay?"

"That would be great, thank you so much, Anita." After they hung up, Jane decided on a shower and fresh clothes. A few minutes before one p.m., she stepped off the elevator in the lobby at the same time Anita came through the door. After exchanging greetings and hugs, the two women went into the coffee shop and ordered their meal. At first, Jane let the conversation flow, catching up on their lives and times since they'd seen each other. After the dishes had been cleared away, and their coffee cups refilled, she got down to business.

"Anita, the reason I called," she began hesitantly, "I have an interesting case at the moment, and I was wondering if you could help me."

"Well, I'll do what I can, but how can I help?"

"My patient is a sixteen-year-old girl who lives in a small town in Washington State. She hit her head on a wall a week ago, and she now seems to be receiving memory signals from someone who died the same night she was born." Anita's eyes widened in surprise.

"Are you talking clairvoyance, E.S.P., or something like that?" She took a sip her coffee. "I wouldn't have thought you were a believer in the paranormal."

"Well, normally I'm not, really. But I haven't been able to explain this one scientifically. My patient drew a sketch of the house she claims to have lived in. I went there today and it's completely accurate. The lawn, the grounds, the neighborhood, everything. She remembers details that only the person who lived there or someone extremely close to that person could know."

"So, she's given you a name to identify who she was?" Anita sounded skeptical.

"Yes, Christina Kingsbury," Jane stated, watching Anita for a reaction. Anita almost choked on her coffee.

"Kingsbury. How did you know to come to me?" Anita tried

to calm herself.

"What do you mean?" Jane was puzzled. She hadn't expected this reaction. "Christina Kingsbury's murder was my first court case with the DA's office, up until then, they had me filing briefs. But when this case came up, Larson wanted a woman at his table, and all the others were on vacation or maternity leave or something, so it came to me."

"How well do you remember the case?" Jane was elated, this was better than she had hoped for.

"You never forget your first murder case," Anita stated emphatically. "It involved a lot of money; her husband killed her."

"Not according to Claire." Jane watched as Anita's eyes narrowed. "She claims that she knew the killer, but that it wasn't her husband, Mike."

"But all the evidence pointed at him. There was almost no defense, and the jury wasn't even out half a day," Anita protested. "He was found guilty and sentenced to life. He's still in prison."

"Claire mentioned that her father didn't like her husband, and that he was rich and powerful. Could he have perhaps swayed the case?" Jane wondered.

"I remember that he was pushing everyone to find out who killed his daughter, he had a lot of political influence. He had helped re-elect both the Senator and the Mayor, so they were more than happy to put pressure on the DA to solve this case." She frowned. "I suppose he could have rushed things, not giving anyone time to find another suspect. Everyone just seemed so sure the husband was guilty. I remember thinking afterwards that it was almost too easy."

"Would there be any possibility of me speaking to Christina's father?"

"No, I'm sorry, he died several years ago. I'm surprised he lived that long after his daughter's death, it seemed to take a lot out of him. David Larson might be able to help you, though, he was the lawyer on the case, and he is now the District Attorney. It would depend entirely on what you want, of course," she reasoned.

"How about the husband?" Jane asked hopefully.

"You mean visit him in prison? What good would that do?"

"Well, I'd like to find some clues about Christina that no one else would know. I'm still testing Claire, I guess. Claire mentioned something several times about her thirtieth birthday party and I was hoping that her husband could give me more information about Christina. I'm curios to know how she would know all this; what if it's real and the wrong man is in prison? I just can't ignore that possibility."

"Hmm, well, I'll make some inquiries, and see what develops. Larson isn't going to be too happy if it turns out we convicted the wrong man sixteen years ago. Meanwhile," she glanced at her watch, "did you need to be somewhere?" Jane also looked at her watch.

"Oh, twenty minutes! Good thing you checked. Thanks for seeing me and being willing to help. I'll wait for your call." They parted with another hug; Jane paid the check and headed off for her meeting. She was sure now that she could find out the truth behind Claire's claims and maybe free an innocent man in the process.

Chapter 7

Jane called her office and left a message on her receptionist's voicemail instructing her to reschedule all her appointments for the next several days because she had been detained in New York on the Warner case. She then called room service and had breakfast sent up to be sure that she would not miss Anita if she called. At about ten thirty a.m., the phone rang.

"Good news!" Anita's jubilant voice rang in Jane's ear.

"I have permission to take you in to visit Mike Kingsbury. Unfortunately, not until tomorrow, are you ok to stay here until then?"

"Yes, I've already arranged to be here for a while. What time tomorrow?" Jane asked.

"I'll pick you up at ten." With that, they ended their call, and, as Jane finished her breakfast, she wondered what she was going to do for the rest of the day. Firmly putting the whole case out of her mind, she put on a floral print sundress and walking shoes and went window-shopping. She had lunch in a trendy restaurant on Second Avenue, checked out the galleries, and walked up and down Broadway reading all the marquees. After a quiet dinner in the hotel coffee shop, she climbed into bed and slept like a log until her alarm woke her.

When Anita arrived, Jane was waiting in the lobby. She had taken care to dress conservatively, since she had no experience walking into prisons. Anita approved her outfit and, with that, they set off, hailing a cab.

"Tell me more about Christina's father," Jane suggested, in the car. "I need to get a clear picture of him, since I can't talk to him."

"Well, he was at the trial every day. I spoke with him several times, he was a very powerful man, what this man wanted, he usually got. He died of heart failure in the fall of '98, the people that attended his funeral read like a 'Who's Who' list."

"If his wife and only daughter were both dead, who arranged the funeral?" Anita chuckled. "It had been pre-arranged in his will. His lawyers had specific instructions for every detail. One thing I do know, he was convinced that Mike was guilty, he made sure our office left no stone unturned in looking for evidence against Mike. In fact, Paul was the one who first told the police about the private investigator, who turned out to be an enormous help. Here we are." Surprised, Jane looked out the window. The drive seemed to have taken no time at all.

They paid the cabbie, signed in at the guard desk, and the guard escorted them to a room where they waited. A few minutes later another door opened and in walked another guard leading a prisoner. Anita recognized him immediately, Mike Kingsbury. He had lost weight and was a little paler than she remembered, but he was still handsome, his charm showing through in the crooked grin that he gave her. "Well, if it isn't the pretty lady lawyer who helped put me in here!" The guard sat him down in a chair then stepped back a few feet. The two women took seats on the other side of the table.

"I was only doing my job, Mr. Kingsbury," Anita started, only to be interrupted.

"Mike, call me Mike. Who is this lovely lady with you?" Mike Kingsbury turned toward Jane with a smile.

"Dr. Jane Radcliff. She's here to ask you a few questions about Christina," Anita leaned back in her seat to allow Mike's attention to focus on Jane.

"Dr.?" Mike seemed puzzled. "A psychiatrist? Did you come here to find out why a fine, upstanding citizen such as myself would suddenly go psycho and kill his wife?" The bitterness was coming through now. "Or have you come to tell me you made a mistake, and you want to make sure I'm not going to go kill the people who put me here?"

"Neither, Mike," Jane said gently, trying to diffuse the situation. "I just need to know a few things. First of all, did you kill your wife?" Mike sighed.

"No, I did not kill my wife. I told everyone that from the beginning. I didn't kill her, I don't know who did, and no matter how long they keep me here, I'll say the same thing. I loved Christina. Her father is the one that made sure I was suspected; I blame him for putting me here; so don't you worry your pretty little head, Counselor, I won't break out of here and come after you," he added, looking at Anita. He was trying to get back the mood he had been in before, but Jane could see it was a struggle. She quietly cleared her throat to get his attention.

"I can't tell you all the details, but there may be a possibility that we can find out who really killed your wife. That's why I need to know Christina's story from you. Please tell me everything you can remember about Christina's thirtieth birthday party." Mike looked at Jane as though trying to read her; he seemed to like what he saw, because he relaxed and closed his eyes for a moment and let his thoughts drift back to Christina's birthday party.

Chapter 8

New York City
Saturday, June 1, 1991
9:00 PM

"No wonder every woman wants to stay twenty nine forever," Christina thought, looking around the room, "so they wouldn't have to endure a party like this one." It was the kind of party filled with all the right people and all the right things, but you leave wondering if you really had fun. Although she wore a flattering gown from the exclusive Oleg Cassini couture line, she felt underdressed and outclassed. Her father had been outrageously extravagant and had obviously gone to great lengths to make this a very special day for her, after all, how many fathers would rent the Grand Ballroom of the Waldorf Astoria and have the connections to arrange for a star like Barry Manilow to perform for her.

"All this just for a birthday party. On the other hand, how many other fathers could afford this?" she smiled to herself.

As the only daughter, and sole heir of tycoon Paul Solderburg, Christina had every luxury available to her. Despite her wealth, Christina was surprisingly understated, perhaps even plain in appearance, while not unattractive, she was rarely referred to as beautiful. Christina's most remarkable characteristics were her large, luminous brown eyes. Even when smiling, her beautiful dark brown eyes fringed with soft long lashes made her appear sad, wistful, and always lonely. Christina's long, dark hair was usually pulled back into a pony tail and tied with a ribbon. Though not exactly stylish, her hair was shiny and luxurious. Christina's use of makeup was minimal, most of the time she would leave home with nothing more than a quick application of moisturizer and a touch of lip gloss. Many had suggested to her that "a little more here and there" would do wonders for her look; her reluctance to take such suggestions was well known. Careful diet and exercise made Christina fit and not without an appealing figure. Her height coupled with a small waist and hips made her appear slender and lithe. Christina chose the most conservative fashions and although they were always perfectly cut from the best fabrics available, the muted tones she preferred only enhanced her often-drab appearance. On occasion, Christina would reluctantly wear a more daring designer creation and have her hair and make-up professionally done. On these rare occasions, Christina shined like a polished gem. Then, admiring eyes would often greet the shy heiress, pleased at her successful attempts at glamour. Her eyes, however, remained the same large pools, betraying her insecurity and loneliness.

"Christina, darling, you look marvelous," came a gushing voice from behind her. She turned to encounter Mrs. Koch, the mayor's wife, with a concerned look on her face. "You look sad, is something wrong?"

"I'm sorry, I was just daydreaming. How nice that you and Mr. Koch could join us tonight. Where is our honorable mayor?" Christina asked, trying to sound polite.

"The last time I saw him, he and your father were discussing the upcoming elections," she answered with a small sigh. "I'm not sure we could pull them apart if we tried." Why on earth would we try, Christina thought wryly, grateful for the break from her father's watchful eye, laughing as was expected of her. There's a pair I'd rather separate, she thought as her eyes scanned the dance floor finding her husband, Mike, dancing entirely too close, for the third - or was it the fourth – time with her best friend Marlene. Except for the first, obligatory, dance with 'the birthday girl', he hadn't been near her all evening. With more than a twinge of jealousy, she watched Marlene's long red hair swing rhythmically back and forth to the live music over the arm Mike had encircling her waist. Mike's Nordic blond hair contrasted well against hers and shone radiantly as the light caught it when he threw his head back, laughing at what Marlene said. How long had it been since he had laughed so freely with her like that? Taking a deep breath, hoping to recover her cool outward appearance, she smiled and turned back to Mrs. Koch.

"Well, let's go find them, anyway. The band's about to take a break, and I suspect Daddy wants me to open my gift before people start going home." But before they left their spot, she heard her father's all too recognizable voice.

"There's my baby girl! Honey, you remember Senator Moynihan and his wife Elizabeth, don't you?" Although her father was smiling, his smile did not quite reach his eyes, instead they were reminding her silently, yet deliberately how she should act in public. She had received just such reminders all of her life, leaving her feeling often like a puppet, dangling from the puppeteer's controlling strings. Christina smiled, nodding and shaking hands with the politically powerful couple. Just then the band announced a break, and Christina's father took her elbow.

"Come on, everyone, I'm going to give my daughter her birthday gift. Where's that husband of yours?"

"Right here, Sir." They turned to see Mike confidently sauntering towards them, Marlene on his arm, her emerald green eyes sparkling with laughter and excitement. As they reached the group, Marlene's husband, Kevin, joined them. Marlene slowly moved to his side, almost reluctantly, it seemed to Christina.

"I have Christina's gift, too," Mike offered, "she can open them both." Paul forced himself not to frown despite the intrusion to his and Christina's spotlight. He didn't care for Mike, but for Christina's sake, he remained cheerful.

"Sure, no problem," he answered. Mike smiled tightly, moving to the other side of Christina, antagonizing the older man still more. The dislike between them was mutual; Paul had objected strongly to their marriage from the start. Mike had always felt he didn't measure up to her father's standards, as Paul was one of the richest, most affluent and powerful men in New York. His son-in-law was wise enough to know it and wise enough to stay in his good graces, at least in public. The entire group of party guests crowded around the stage where Christina, Mike and Paul were, trying to get a glimpse of what Paul was giving his daughter for her birthday.

"Ladies and gentlemen, may I have your attention please? I want to thank all of you for coming out tonight to celebrate my little girl's birthday, though, she doesn't look like a little girl anymore." Christina blushed slightly at this. "I would especially like to thank Senator Moynihan and his wife, as well as the Honorable Ed Koch and his wife, for taking time off from their election campaigns to be here." There was a smattering of soft polite laughter. It was no secret that Solderburg, Ltd. had contributed heavily to both campaigns.

"I would now like to present my daughter with her gift. Since she was a baby, I have given her a pearl every year. This year, I decided it was time for a new gem." He took a rich blue velvet box from his pocket, and ceremoniously handed it to Christina. Even from a distance, the guests could recognize the box as being from the most fashionable well-known New York jewelers. As she opened it, lifting the lid slowly, the flash of light reflected off of the necklace inside. The remarkable beauty and extravagance of his gift made everyone who could see, gasp. It was unquestionably the most exquisite diamond necklace Christina had ever seen. The sparkle from the stones was nearly blinding.

"Oh, Daddy, it's marvelous," she breathed, her voice full of excitement. He took the necklace out of the box, placed it around her neck, and fastened the intricate clasp. She turned to show Mike, nearly knocking the box he was holding out of his hand. Catching it, in one smooth athletic motion, he handed it to her.

"Happy birthday, Honey," he said. She opened the box to reveal a pair of diamond earrings that matched the necklace almost perfectly. Laughing gaily, she said, "Did you two go shopping together?" A small murmur went through the crowd; the feud between the two men was no secret. Christina quickly removed the earrings she was wearing and slipped them into Mike's pocket. She then put on the new ones and turned to show the crowd. The sparkling gems were the perfect foil for her rich brown hair and brown eyes. Applause erupted, but Christina wasn't sure if they were applauding her gifts, or the fact that the band was returning at last to the stage. The crowd began heading for the dance floor, and as the music began, Christina turned to Mike hopefully, to see if he would dance with her, she was too late; he was already heading quickly for the floor with another young and beautiful woman. Oh, well, she thought bitterly, that's what I get for marrying a younger man. All the happiness she had felt a moment ago vanished. Christina glanced at her watch; it was only eleven-thirty. How she wished she could gracefully end this party and just go home. Then her eye caught a group exchanging good-byes at the front entrance of the hotel, it seemed the Mayor and his wife were calling it an evening. She hurried over to shake hands and thank them again for coming. The Mayor's departure seemed to be the signal for everyone to leave, and thank god for that, she thought, as her face felt as if it would crack from the smile she'd held for so long.

"Well, sweetheart, did you enjoy the party?" her father asked gently, just as he did every year. He reached to hug her, and his white beard tickled her cheek, making her feel like a child again, safe, warm, and loved very much.

"Daddy, it was a wonderful party, as always, thank you, but you really shouldn't go overboard like this," she protested.

"Nonsense! It isn't every day my baby girl turns thirty, is it?" Smiling broadly with pride, he kissed her on the cheek. "Goodnight, kitten, I'll come by and see you next week sometime."

Chapter 9

As Christina and Mike finally exited the building, an elegant Mercedes-Benz limousine pulled out of the valet lot and headed around the curved driveway approaching the hotel's magnificent lobby entrance. As it stopped in front of the Kingsbury's, the doorman courteously opened the back door and wished the couple a good evening.

"Happy birthday, Mrs. Kingsbury," he added, admiration clearly present in his tone. He was immediately rewarded by a warm thank you from Christina, even though Mike was hustling her into the car.

"Where to, Ma'am?" the limousine driver, Steven Mallock asked as he turned to look back at the couple.

"Home, please, Stephen," Christina answered as Mike gritted his teeth. Mike didn't miss the insult in the driver's habit of only addressing Christina with questions when needing any sort of direction.

The chauffeur and the housekeeper, who was most likely waiting up for them at home, were a wedding gift from Christina's father, and always seemed to make it clear that they worked for her, not him. It was a subtle reminder of the popular public opinion that Christina had married outside her class, below the station to which she was born. Never mind that he was a successful architect; he hadn't inherited the money, he actually worked for a living. To be snubbed by this earring-sporting handyman made him furious. Christina sat quietly, remembering the evening.

"Did you have a good time tonight, Mike?" Christina asked.

He turned his head, his blue eyes disguising what had been going through his mind.

"Oh, sure, great party," he said. "It's amazing what money in the right places can do," he noted sarcastically. She bit her lip instead of retorting, she knew better. She had no intention of starting a fight by defending her father.

"I'm sorry I didn't spend more time with you tonight, Honey. The music sounded so good, I just couldn't get off the dance floor, and I know you don't like to dance much," he offered as an explanation for his behavior. She almost laughed out loud. She loved to dance – with him, just to have the chance to be in his arms, but when was the last time he had asked?

"It's ok," Christina lied. "After all, we had to make sure everyone had a good time," she said, trying to hide her bitterness.

"Are you upset about something, Honey?" he inquired solicitously.

"No," she lied again, "just tired. After all, I'm a year older today." Her light tone did not match the dark mood creeping up inside her. Mike smiled at the joke, and they both fell into a grateful silence.

As they pulled through the iron gates into the driveway, Christina marveled, as always, at the grandeur of her home. Despite a life of advantage, she would never learn to take wealth for granted, as her father – and yes, even Mike – did. Graceful, white columns and a full veranda reminiscent of the old charming South greeted them as they drove up the curved driveway to the front of the house. She pictured it as it appeared in daylight and could see the perfectly manicured lawns and a profusion of flowers, maintained daily by a troop of experienced landscapers. The flowers were her greatest joy; they never failed to fill the air with impossible color and heavenly fragrance. Pulling up in front of the portico, Steven hurried around and opened the car door.

"Will you be needing anything else tonight, Ma'am?"

"No thank you Steven, just take the gifts out of the trunk and put them in the foyer. Tomorrow is soon enough for carting them upstairs. You may put the car away for the night and go home."

"Very good, Ma'am," he answered, closing the car door firmly and heading around to the back. As they ascended the grand front steps, Christina reached into Mike's jacket pocket and pulled out her earrings as well as the box from her new ones, Mike also pulled her necklace box out of the other pocket and handed it to her. He reached for the doorknob, but Nancy, the housekeeper, who had indeed been waiting for the sound of the car arriving, opened the door from within.

"You're home early, Ma'am, is everything alright?" she appeared concerned.

"Yes, Nancy, it was a wonderful party. The mayor left early, and that seemed to break things up. We do appreciate your waiting up; however, we won't be needing anything tonight. Steven is going to leave my gifts here, and we will put them away tomorrow. We'll be sleeping late, I expect." Christina stifled a small yawn.

"Actually, Honey, I have to go into the office tomorrow," said Mike, contradicting Christina. "The design on that new library project needs to be reworked and printed in time for the meeting Monday afternoon. Please don't bother fixing breakfast for me Nancy, I'll eat downtown, even though it won't be nearly as good." He quickly added hoping to gain the favor of the disapproving servant.

"Yes, sir," she answered, smiling reluctantly at the compliment, "I'll see you in the morning then, Ma'am."

"Good night, Nancy," Christina replied and started up the spiral staircase that dominated the space just beyond the foyer.

"I didn't know you had to work tomorrow, Mike." Christina appeared dejected.

"I didn't know myself until Friday afternoon," he said, "and I didn't want to spoil your party by bringing it up today. This will give you a chance to invite Marlene over to ooh and aah over your gifts without me around." It seemed to Christine she was doing a lot these days without him around, but again she bit her lip.

"Good idea," she said. "I'll call Marlene after breakfast."

Entering the master bedroom, Christina was once again struck by the luxury of her surroundings. One wall was half taken up by a mammoth gray and brown marble fireplace. Deep luxurious carpet covered the floor; it was the finest of carpets, the type that made you want to kick off your shoes and curl your toes in it, which she did with great relief. It was almost like being on the beach, without the nuisance or mess of sand in your shoes, she thought with a smile. Stepping into her walk-in closet, she was greeted by glittering reflections of herself in her flawless designer gown. She carefully removed the dress and put on her robe. As she came out, she heard Mike humming one of the popular tunes that had been playing tonight.

"I wish I had kept up with my dancing lessons like Marlene did," she said lightly. "She's quite a good dancer, isn't she? Judge Thames made sure she excelled in the social graces." Mike stopped humming and fixed her with a quizzical look.

"Good grief, Christina, don't tell me you are jealous of Marlene? She's your best friend!" he sounded shocked.

"Yes, but she's so much prettier than I am..." she replied, feeling embarrassed. Her voice trailed off as Mike crossed the room and took her in his arms as she had hoped he would, she had longed for the warmth of him all evening.

"Don't be silly, Christine, you are every bit as pretty, and I've never had any complaints about your dancing, either. I just assumed you didn't like to dance. Did it bother you so much that I danced with her?" He asked, trying to reassure her.

"No, of course not, I was just making conversation. Please let's not argue about it." Christina moved out of his arms over to her dressing table; glancing at her reflection in the mirror, she grimaced, seeing as always, the looks that never quite measured up to her beautiful mother. Taking off her necklace, she placed it in its box and walked over to the large safe in the wall opposite the fireplace. Opening it, she set the box inside.

"What about the earrings?" Mike reminded her as she started to close the safe.

"No," she said, "I'll be wearing those again right away." She took the earrings off and put them in the original box, placing it on the corner of the dressing table. She went into her bathroom to get ready for bed and when she returned, Mike was already under the covers with his eyes closed.

"I love you, Mike." she whispered, crawling into bed.

"I love you, too, Honey. Happy birthday." Turning toward her, he took her in his arms and she drifted off to sleep, feeling that same warm and safe feeling she had earlier with her father.

Chapter 10

Christina's fingers touched the earring box on her dressing table. Her mind drifted back to the party, and again she saw Mike dancing with one young, lovely girl after another, even her own best friend, Marlene Endicott. She thought about how they had met and become best friends all those years ago. She was ten, Marlene, her junior, only six. Her father and Judge Thames had become great friends, and the two of them were flung together, without consideration for their age difference. Eventually, they became as close as sisters, nothing would break this bond, they thought. Then Mike Kingsbury entered the picture, tall and slim, movie-star handsome with blond hair and blue eyes. Marlene had made no secret of the fact that she envied Christina. Her own marriage was not happy, and she was constantly comparing her husband, Kevin, to Mike, not only in looks but also in charm and personality. Suddenly, the phone on Christina's dressing table rang, and she jumped, knocking the earring box to the floor.

"Hello?" she said, reaching for the box and the phone at the same time.

"Christina," Marlene's familiar, bubbly voice exclaimed, "I'm so glad you are home. You don't have any plans today, do you? Kevin is in his study all wrapped up in a case that goes to court tomorrow, and I'm bored stiff. Let's go shopping or something." Christina smiled. Shopping was the cure-all for Marlene. It was a good thing Judge Thames had left her a wealthy woman, or there would be no way Kevin could support her.

"Sure," she answered. "Come on over, we can brunch and plan our attack on Manhattan."

As Marlene pulled up in front of the house, Steven, Christina's chauffeur and handy man walked out of the front door.

"Good morning, Mrs. Endicott," he said respectfully. "Mrs. Kingsbury is in the garden, and asks that you join her there." He held the door open in invitation, so she could step through.

"Thank you, Steven," Marlene said automatically. She made her way toward the back of the house. As she stepped out into the spectacular garden, she greeted Christina.

"Steven hardly needed to tell me where you were. Where else would you be when it's not raining?" Both women laughed at this, knowing it was true, as they kissed each other's cheeks in the European fashion.

"I do love my garden," Christina smiled affectionately while looking around at her flowers. "I think it's my favorite place in the world. I wish it weren't illegal to be buried in one's own back yard." Marlene shivered.

"Ooh, don't talk about death on a beautiful day like today, I mean, you're only thirty!" She laughed off the feeling and sat down, reaching for a glass of lemonade. "You've only got four years on me, and I still feel like a child sometimes." Christina looked at her friend closely. She could see lines on her face that weren't there a few days ago.

"What's wrong, Marlene?" she asked. "Shopping isn't really what brought you here today." Sighing heavily, Marlene put down her drink. She stared down at her hands, perfectly manicured as always.

"I never could keep anything from you, could I? Kevin has received a job offer in Boston. I didn't even know he was looking, and now he says he wants us to move there." She looked back up at Christina, her eyes now two green pools of unshed tears. "I don't want to leave New York! This is my home. I grew up here, all my friends are here, everything I know. I'll bet Mike would never just up and want you to move without at least talking it over with you." Christina smiled tightly.

"Well, no, it's not likely. But Mike has a partnership in his

46

business, and can control re-locating issues. Kevin isn't even a partner in that firm. Maybe he has more chance for advancement in Boston. You should at least hear his reasons for moving before you veto the idea, after all, you took the same vows I did: for better or worse." She tried to sound logical, but inside she was thinking the distance would be good for both marriages.

"You sound almost as if you want me to go," pouted Marlene, disappointed by her friend's lack of concern.

"Oh, don't be silly, I will miss you terribly, and you know it. Now, please, let's talk about something else. Do you have any plans for the fourth of July?" For the rest of the visit, Christina managed to keep the conversation light, and as a result, Marlene left in much better spirits than when she arrived.

Chapter 11

Mike's Porsche roared down the drive and through the gates, and Christina breathed a sigh of relief. This morning would not be a good day for him to work from home since her father was coming for breakfast. Christina's father, at age 60, still drew the open admiration of women wherever he went, almost like an older movie star; he possessed a tanned, still-handsome face and sparkling blue eyes. Paul laughed often, revealing perfectly straight, incredibly white teeth. Despite a great deal of speculation that they were capped, his flawless smile was just as nature had given him. Paul kept his soft white hair and beard trimmed close, the short haircut and beard only accentuated the appearance of casual elegance; he was a wealthy man, and it showed in his good looks and confident carriage. Many men envied Paul, and still more women wondered what life would be like as his partner in romance. When Paul's limousine arrived, Christina was predictably in the garden with her coffee. As he passed through the house, Nancy took his coat, and assured him that breakfast would be served shortly. He greeted Christina with a warm, affectionate kiss on the cheek, while asking how she was.

"Just fine, Daddy," she answered. "Isn't this an absolutely glorious morning?"

"It certainly is," he agreed heartily. "Did Mike go to work this morning?"

"He goes to work every morning, Daddy, don't start with the scrutiny and criticism of him, ok? Not everyone grows up with the same advantages I had. After all, I had both my parents until..."

"I know, I know," interrupted Christina's father, "'poor Mike, his father died when he was young, he grew up in boarding schools' – I've heard the whole sob story, kitten. But it's not the past that builds your character, it's how you overcome the obstacles in life that counts, and Mike seems to prefer to skate around them, that's all."

"You can't argue with the success of his business. He has clients all over the country; you don't get that by being lazy. If he married me for my money, he would have quit working; instead, he has work harder than ever since we got married. Probably just to prove all the rumors wrong."

"Well, I do have to admit he's no slouch as an architect. But I don't trust him as far as women are concerned. He's going to break your heart, I just know it," he predicted.

"Daddy, please, if all you are going to do is trash Mike, you can have your breakfast elsewhere!" This outburst came just as Nancy stepped through the door with the breakfast tray, and she stopped, undecided whether to intrude or not. Christina was on the verge of tears, and her father quickly hugged her and apologized.

"Don't cry, baby, we can change the subject, I didn't come over to upset you." Christina motioned to Nancy to serve breakfast and conversation was put on hold while Christina and her father busied themselves with their meal. When they were finished eating, Paul leaned back in his chair.

"I wish your mother were still here," he said. "She always had a way of putting into words what I was thinking, but in a much gentler way. You know I'm just trying to look after you like she would have, don't you, baby girl?" he pleaded for her to understand.

"I understand, Daddy," Christina rose and kissed his cheek, "let's not fight about it. I love Mike and he loves me, and it shouldn't concern anyone else."

"Yes, but you always tend to think with your heart, and not your head." Her father rose and picked up his briefcase. He smoothed down the front of his expertly tailored suit and smiled at her. "Well, I have a meeting, and can't be late. I enjoyed breakfast, sweetheart, we'll do it again soon, I hope." Christina smiled and nodded, then watched him walk back into the house. She turned back to her garden, thinking about what her father had said about Mike and women. She had been quick to defend him, but hadn't she had the same thoughts herself? Maybe she and Mike should talk.

As Paul was leaving, he saw Steven polishing the car, and went to talk with him. Steven, a twenty-five year old man, six feet tall, a ring in his right ear, lived with his invalid mother; Paul hired him as a chauffeur and a handyman for Christina. Polite and punctual, Steven was also a hard worker.

"Steven, remember when I sent you here, I asked you to keep an eye on my daughter?"

"Yes, sir." Steven replied, nodding, causing a lock of coal-black hair over his forehead. "Is there something wrong?"

"That's what I'd like to know. Does she seem happy still?" Steven toyed with his earring and considered the question a moment.

"Yes, sir, they seem very content with each other."

"I don't want content, I want happy. You keep an eye out, and let me know if things go awry."

"Yes, sir, will do," Steven answered respectfully. On the way to the office, Paul thought about his conversation with his daughter. She had been such a happy child, in fact, she had always been happy, until her mother died. It had been Mike who appeared to have brought that happiness back into her. Maybe he was just envious that he hadn't been able to pull her out of the depression himself. Maybe he was wrong about Mike, but he doubted it.

Chapter 12

No wonder they call these "bored" meetings, Mike thought, barely suppressing a smile, thinking his joke was rather clever. The city official had been talking for nearly an hour, and Mike could hardly remember a word. He tried to focus, knowing how important it was to get this contract – a new municipal swimming pool. Suddenly, his senses were on full alert, a woman had walked into the room, one who could easily grace the covers of a fashion magazine. She moved her tall slender frame with the quiet dignity and grace of a dancer. Her tailored clothes were in subdued, tasteful colors designed to set off her blond hair and big blue eyes to perfection. In Mike Kingsbury's estimation she was perfect.

"Ah, Miss Brown, there you are!" The city official seemed just as relieved to stop talking, as Mike was to stop listening. "Mike Kingsbury, I'd like you to meet Judith Brown. She is the architectural coordinator for the city. She'll be working with you on this project." It was only then that Mike realized the contract was theirs even without his alert attention. "She will be organizing all your permits and such, making sure you stay on time and under budget." He laughed heartily at his own joke, but Mike and Judy were busy shaking hands and murmuring greetings, their eyes already meeting and sharing a secret. "Now, Judith, suppose we all sit down and go over..."

"I don't think that will be necessary," Judy interrupted smoothly. "I have already gone over the specs, as I'm sure Mike – may I call you Mike? – has." She barely waited for Mike's nod before she laid a delicate hand on his arm and began leading him to a table. "We can handle this on our own, I'm sure. I wouldn't want to keep you from important city business, Councilman."

"Yes, yes, of course," the Councilman found himself agreeing almost against his will. "Well, I'll leave you two to work then." Neither of them noticed his departure.

Over the next two months, Mike and Judy made many excuses to see each other. Because they both had an interest in architecture, Mike found Judy an intellectual equal and easy to talk to. He found himself talking about long forgotten topics like his childhood, his fears, and even his dreams. He had never been able to open up to Christina this way. He silently thanked his lucky stars that had assigned Judy to this particular project, it was almost as if fate stepped in and they were meant to meet. Since the pool was such an important, high profile project for the city, no one raised any eyebrows at the amount of time the two of them spent together. A lunch meeting that spilled over into the afternoon, Saturday mornings in one office or the other. If only a fraction of the time was spent talking about the pool, who was to know? The occasional twinge of guilt either of them may have felt was instantly shrugged off, after all, it's not like they were having an affair; they just enjoyed each other's company, right? Mike had never even considered cheating on Christina, as much as he flirted with women, but now, he found himself wondering what it would be like. Judy was so beautiful, what if...Stop it! he admonished himself. You're a married man, and don't you forget who your father–in–law is. If Paul even knew he was having these thoughts, he'd move heaven and earth to put an end to the marriage that he was never happy about in the first place. And then where would you be? Every time he saw Judy, all logic went out the window, he never grew tired of looking at her, he considered her more beautiful, perhaps even more perfect, every day; sometimes, he was afraid she would see the desire in his eyes. As time wore on, however, he began to want her to see it, and to reciprocate.

Chapter 13

The groundbreaking ceremony was scheduled for the day before Halloween. The air was crisp and clear, characteristic of New York in autumn. Tuesday afternoon, the architectural team had met with city officials to assure them that everything was proceeding as planned and was on schedule. As Judy left the room, she brushed by Mike and slipped a folded piece of paper into his coat pocket with a wink. Excited by her covert action, he hurried back to the privacy of his office; he pulled out the note and unfolded it.

"Meet me for lunch tomorrow; no business allowed," it read. He picked up the phone and dialed her office.

"Where and when?" he asked eagerly when she answered.

"Marion's at noon," she answered. "We should be finished with the ceremony and press conference by then."

"I'll be there." Hanging up the phone, he looked again at the note. He especially liked the "no business" part. Grinning, he put the note back in his pocket.

The morning of the ceremony, Mike was up and dressed earlier than usual. He tried to tell himself that he was dressing with care for the television cameras, but deep inside he knew better. Christina rolled over and asked sleepily if he wanted her to go to the ceremony with him. He assured her that it was unnecessary, and she gratefully rolled over and went back to sleep.

That was close, Mike thought. How would he meet Judy for lunch if Christina came along? He thought about the wording of the note she had slipped him. Obviously, she was ready to take this relationship farther, how could he let her know he wholeheartedly agreed? As he turned toward his closet, his eye fell upon the familiar blue velvet box on Christina's dressing table. Earrings! The perfect gift for a lady. They were not too pretentious, yet a definite token of more than friendship, and he definitely had more than friendship in mind. He would go to the jewelry store...wait; there wouldn't be time, the stores didn't open until ten, and he had to be at the ceremony. The press conference afterwards would take him right up to meeting Judy at noon. Looking again at the box on Christina's table, he tried to remember the last time that he had seen her wear those earrings, New Year's Eve, certainly, to match the necklace, but since then? Mike walked to his closet and pulled on his coat. Then, with one eye on Christina's sleeping form, he casually walked by the dressing table and adeptly slipped the box into his pocket, rearranging a few things so that the absence of the diamond earrings would not be immediately noticeable.

At the ceremony, he could hardly keep his mind on business; he was imagining Judy's reaction to the gift. She looks stunning today, he thought to himself, simply ravishing. As Mayor Koch dug the shovel into the dirt, cameras flashed, and Mike backed up a step acting as though they were blinding him. In reality, he caught Judy's eye behind the mayor's back, and winked, meaningfully. She gave him a small secret smile in return, also full of hidden meaning; noon couldn't come too quickly for either of them. When he was finally able to break way from the press, he made his way to Marion's, arriving a few minutes after the appointed time. The maitre d' showed him to the table at which Judy was already seated.

"Miss Brown, I hope I haven't kept you waiting?" he said formally, for the benefit of the restaurant staff, rumored to eavesdrop at every opportunity. With a twinkle in her eye, Judy answered just as formally,

"Not at all, Mr. Kingsbury, I arrived only minutes ago myself." The maitre d' left, and they smiled at each other like two schoolchildren playing hooky. The conversation was kept light and, as agreed, no business was discussed. Time passed much too quickly, and soon it was time for them both to go back to work.

"Oh! I almost forgot!" Mike exclaimed as he was helping Judy on with her coat. He reached into his own coat pocket, explaining, "I brought you a little gift. A small token of my appreciation for all your hard work." Then, so quietly that only she could hear, he added, "and also of my affection."

"But I was only doing my job," she protested – not very convincingly – as she reached for the box. The gasp of delight when she opened it, however, was genuine.

"Mike! You shouldn't have," she said quietly, in an alluring, breathy whisper. "They're far too much. We have to be careful; rumors could damage both our careers, not to mention your marriage."

"Nonsense!" he said briskly. His confidence was rising. "Friends are allowed to buy each other gifts." He shrugged into his coat and led Judy out of the restaurant. "We need to do this more often, especially the 'no business' part."

"Oh, I agree." she said, taking a deep breath.

They left the restaurant and returned to their jobs, both excited and hopeful, thinking of the future, and wondering what it would bring.

Chapter 14

Halloween, thought Christina, as she rolled out of bed. She remembered the parties her parents used to host when she was a child. Fancy dresses, often disguising her as a princess or fairy, beautiful masks, and glittering jewelry. With that thought, she reached for her earring box, reminding herself that it was time they went into the safe. Frowning, she noticed the disarray on her dressing table, and there was no sign of the box, she could have sworn she left it there. She carefully moved things around, thinking she had simply buried the box. Recalling how she had knocked it off more than once, she looked down on the floor, and then behind the table. Now she was genuinely worried; hadn't they been there last night? Thinking back, she couldn't be certain. She tried to recall the last time she had worn them. Was it to lunch at Marlene's for Labor Day? Nearly two months ago! She should have put them in the safe every night; Mike had reminded her many times. He was not going to be pleased. Unless...? She went to the safe, opening it quickly. No, he hadn't put them away for her. Surely, he would not have hidden them just to teach her a lesson; he was not a cruel person. She left the room, agitated.

"Nancy!" She called down the stairs.

"Yes, Ma'am?" Nancy came to the bottom of the stairs, duster in hand. "Breakfast is ready and waiting for you."

"Thank you, Nancy, but I need to ask you something first." she said, worry in her voice. "Have you seen the earrings my husband gave me for my birthday? I seem to have misplaced them."

"Perhaps Mr. Kingsbury put them in the safe?" Nancy suggested in an attempt to be helpful. Christina shook her head.

"Well, I wouldn't worry, they'll turn up. I'll keep an eye out while I'm cleaning. I'm sure I saw the box on your dressing table a few days ago, they can't be too far."

"I hope you're right," Christina sighed. It wouldn't do any good to agonize over them. She went down to breakfast, pondering the mystery while she ate. Throughout the day, she would occasionally think of somewhere they might be, but they were never there. Mike didn't come home for dinner, and the later he was, the more time Christina had to worry about his reaction. When he finally got home, Christina ran to him and hugged him, exclaiming,

"Mike! You're finally home!"

"Sorry, Honey, but you know how important that pool project is to the firm, and we still have to keep up with the other projects we've got going, too."

"I wasn't criticizing, Mike, I just..." Christina bit her lip and turned away so Mike couldn't see the tears forming in her eyes. "I can't find the earrings you gave me for my birthday. I've looked everywhere. I just can't believe I could be so careless!"

Damn! Mike thought to himself. I forgot to buy the earrings!

"I'm sure they're somewhere, Honey," he said tenderly. "Maybe you left them at Marlene's, or your father's house?"

"Maybe," she said, wiping her now teary brown eyes. "I'll ask them both tomorrow. Thank you for not being angry with me."

"Over a pair of earrings? I love you too much for that." He gathered her into his outstretched arms so she could not see the guilt in his eyes. Christina's eyes were closed, she felt so content and grateful for any sign of affection and concern, so rare, it seemed, lately.

The next morning, both Kingsburys were up early; Christina had a breakfast date with her father. There was little conversation as both readied themselves for the day ahead. As they walked down the stairs, however, Mike spoke.

"What are you planning after you see your father?" He fervently hoped the question sounded casual enough.

"I had planned to go shopping with Marlene, but she wasn't feeling well the other day, so we may not be able to. I told her to call me after lunch. Meanwhile, I thought I'd make some plans for the holidays."

Not much time, he thought, I'll have to be there right when the store opens.

"Good idea, Honey, time always goes so fast this time of year." As they reached the bottom of the stairs, Mike got an idea. Carefully, he placed his briefcase under the hall table, then went to the front closet and took out Christina's coat. He helped her on with it, then reached for his own.

"Well, Honey, you have a good time with your father." He needed to distract her so that she would not point out that he was forgetting his briefcase. "We should have him over to dinner soon." Christina's eyes widened. The holiday season was certainly having a positive effect on Mike this year. He put an arm around her shoulders as they walked out the front door. When they reached her car, he kissed her on the cheek.

"See you tonight," he said.

Later that morning, Mike came back in the front door, moving quietly, so as not to alert Nancy, and made his way upstairs to the bedroom. He picked up his hairbrush and walked over to Christina's dressing table. Opening one of the drawers, he pulled a small jeweler's box from his pocket and placed it behind some of the objects inside. He then pushed everything back and placed his hairbrush in the front of the drawer. As he closed the drawer, he could hear footsteps in the hall. Crossing the room quickly, he pretended to be looking through his closet.

"Mr. Kingsbury!" blurted Nancy, a little out of breath still from climbing the stairs. "You startled me!"

"Sorry, Nancy, but I forgot my briefcase this morning, and I can't seem to find it." Closing the closet door, he moved around the room, as though he was still searching.

"It's downstairs under the hall table, Mr. Kingsbury, didn't your secretary give you my message?" Mike thought quickly.

"I had a breakfast meeting this morning, and haven't been to the office yet," he said. "It was only when I reached for it after breakfast that I noticed it missing. I'd better run, I'm late for the next meeting already." Feeling like he'd had a narrow escape, he hurried away.

That evening at dinner and afterwards, Mike seemed determined to cheer Christina up, he cracked jokes, and regaled her with stories from work.

"Honey, have you seen my hairbrush?" he asked her in what he hoped sounded like a casual question, as they got ready for bed.

"No, Mike, I haven't," she answered. "Did you leave it in the bathroom?"

"Not in mine," he said. "Maybe Nancy put it in yours by mistake." He started searching the room, starting with Christina's bath. He checked both closets, and his dressing table. Pretending to be frustrated, he began slamming drawers and muttering. When he came to Christina's dressing table, he grabbed a drawer and gave it a hard yank. The drawer came out completely, scattering its contents everywhere.

"Mike!" Christina was aghast. "It's only a hairbrush, what's wrong with you?" She began picking things up, finding the hairbrush just under the bedspread. "Here it is, it wasn't in my dressing table at all."

"Look, Mike!" she gasped. "My earrings! I wonder why I didn't see them when I was looking earlier." She frowned for a moment, then her face cleared. "Maybe they were too far back. Thank you for discovering them, even if it was an accident." Smiling, she kissed him on the cheek and turned to the safe. As she placed the earring box next to the one containing her necklace, she hesitated, frozen at her discovery. The box containing her lost earrings was not from the same jeweler. She thought back to her party, and distinctly remembered joking with Mike about going shopping with her father. She could clearly remember the amusement the guests found in her suggestion that they would even consider such a thing.

What a sweetheart, she thought. He knew how upset I was about losing those earrings, and he bought new ones! If I find the originals, I will just take these back. After closing the safe, she slipped into bed. Kissing Mike on the cheek, she snuggled up against him and closed her eyes. Mike smiled to himself in the dark as he drifted off to sleep. She felt safe against Mike's chest, and Mike felt secure in his newfound confidence.

The success of the earring switch seemed to make Mike bolder, he spent more and more time with Judy; less and less time at home. He was even taking her to movies and plays, always introducing her as an associate. If he was asked about Christina, he always had a ready reply: she was sick, with her father, or had already seen this, and so on. The holidays, usually a joyful time for Mike, were this year viewed as an interruption; he had to spend them with Christina, and couldn't see Judy. Because he felt a little guilty about this attitude, he was especially thoughtful and considerate, and Christina suspected nothing. She thought often during the holiday season that it might end up being their best ever.

Chapter 15

How time flies, Christina thought as she looked at the calendar. Winter was over, and her beloved garden was beginning to bloom. More buds opened daily revealing the familiar hues of red, pink and oranges, their colors and fragrances reminding her of happier times. She thought about what she would do with the day looming ahead, and suddenly realized how long it had been since she and Mike had spent any real time together. When was the last time they had actually had fun together? He seemed to relax over the holidays, and be home and happy, but since the New Year had started, he was working harder than ever. She tried to recall if her father had made any comments about his work ethic, something that would make him think he had to prove something, but she decided it was this pool project. The city wanted it completed before the school year was over, and Mike must be working against some awful deadlines. She couldn't even remember the last time they had gone out in the evening. If she went to a movie or play, it had been with Marlene or her father. I'll call him, she decided. I'll tell him I'm coming into town to shop, and ask him to meet me for lunch. It's been ages since we've done that. She went to the phone and dialed Mike's office. His secretary, as politely as possible, informed her that Mike was in a meeting and had asked not to be disturbed.

"If it's very important, Mrs. Kingsbury, I'm sure he won't mind my buzzing you in," she offered.

"No, don't interrupt the meeting," Christina said. "Just ask him to call me as soon as it's over, will you?" She was assured that he would call, and hung up the phone. Going to her closet, she tried to find an outfit that would open Mike's eyes and put a little spark back into their marriage. How long had it been since his eyes lit up when she walked into a room? While she was considering and rejecting possibilities, Nancy walked in.

"Excuse me, ma'am," She seemed surprised to find Christina still in the room. "I was just going to gather Mr. Kingsbury's winter suits for the cleaners. I can come back later."

"No, Nancy, it's alright, you go ahead. I'll just step into the shower."

As Christina stepped back into the room, she saw that Nancy had placed a pile of papers – from Mike's pockets – on his dressing table, and a few of them had fallen to the floor landing in the open, clearly in view. Bending down to pick them up, she caught a glimpse of one paper's strange shade of green, it was unfamiliar to her, and it contrasted dramatically amongst the mostly white pile. Her curiosity got the better of her, and she pulled out the note and unfolded it. Across the top was printed "A Note From Judy", and written in decidedly feminine handwriting were the words "Meet me for lunch tomorrow, no business allowed." Spurred on by the shock and surprise of her first discovery, she began to search through the other papers. Her search produced incriminating restaurant receipts, credit card slips for movie tickets, even plays that Mike had told her he was not interested in seeing. She noticed they were all on the same credit card, one she had never seen before, and one in Mike's name only. If these were business related, they would be on his corporate card. Instead, this was a brand new card with his office for an address. Her heart pounding, she picked up the phone again and started to dial. No, calm down, she told herself, he'll call when his meeting is over, and you can ask him to come home. She proceeded to get dressed, after pushing all the papers into a drawer. When Mike had not called by noon, she called again.

"I'm sorry, Mrs. Kingsbury, he just left for lunch," his secretary said.

"Didn't you give him my message this morning?" Christina

could barely keep the anger out of her voice.

"Yes, Ma'am," the secretary said, sounding a little hurt, "I gave it to him as soon as he left the meeting. He was late for a lunch appointment, and said he would take care of it when he got back."

"I'm sorry," Christina took a deep breath, "I shouldn't have snapped at you. I just wanted to, well...never mind. Thank you." She hung up the phone in utter distress, close to tears. She called to Nancy that she would be eating at home after all, then wandered out to her garden to think. Her faithful flowers provided none of their usual solace or relief from the rising suspicion.

What happened to us? she mused dejectedly. Sitting in her favorite chair, she leaned back and closed her eyes, remembering the night she first met Mike. She had accompanied her father to the opening of an art gallery. Solderburg, Ltd. had donated a large sum of money to the gallery, and Paul and Christina were guests of honor. As they arrived, the host had taken them over to introduce them to the architects for the building. As she shook hands politely, she was startled by a grip that did not immediately let go. She looked up into cool clear eyes, the bluest she had ever seen. Eyes that were definitely approving of what they, in turn, saw in her. She had never received such open admiration nor had she ever seen such desire in a man's eyes, not when they looked at her, anyway. Her father, however, was not nearly so approving. When their dating became more serious, he tried to talk her into having Mike investigated.

"After all, a girl can't be too careful these days. Look at the way he dresses; he's obviously living beyond his means, and he's after your money." Maybe if she had listened...no! She had to stop thinking like this. Better to put it out of her mind for now, and confront Mike when he got home. Walking back into the house, she called Marlene in Boston. She would spend the afternoon listening to someone else's problems, and perhaps forget about her own.

That night, Mike was home in time for dinner.

"Mike, did you ever get my phone message today?" Christina said, as casually as she could, as they started on the main course.

"Oh, Honey, I'm sorry!" Mike exclaimed. "My morning meeting went long, making me late for my lunch appointment. I meant to call when I got back to the office! Was it important?"

"Not really," she said carefully. "I was going to come into town for lunch, but since you had a meeting anyway..."

"Yes," he said. "With the architectural coordinator for the pool."

"Oh, how is the pool project going? I always thought it was strange to start construction just before winter started." Mike looked puzzled, then his face cleared. "Oh, that's right, you missed the ground-breaking." He managed to make it sound as if she should have been there, even though he himself had told her it wasn't necessary. "We used an existing building. Gutted it out, brought the structure up to code, now we're building the pool inside it."

"Oh," she said quietly. "So, is Judy a new member of the firm?"

Mike paused with his fork halfway to his mouth. Setting it down carefully, he picked up his napkin and wiped his mouth.

"Judy? Who is Judy?" he said, just as quietly.

"I don't know exactly," Christina stated, wiping her fingers daintily on her own napkin. "It's just a name I saw on a piece of paper. Nancy took your suits to the cleaners today, and she emptied out your pockets, there was a note from Judy about lunch."

"Oh! Miss Brown," Mike chuckled, "On one of her little green desk notes?" He was overdoing it, Christine thought.

"She is the Architectural Coordinator I had lunch with today, she works for the City, very important to the project, handles the permits and such." His casual tone was forced, and Christina could sense tension in his normally relaxed speech.

"I see," said Christina. She saw all too clearly. Apparently Mike didn't remember the "no business" written on the note. Or was this one of several such notes? What further proof did she need? She excused herself, pleading a headache. She fled the room moments before bursting into tears. When Mike came upstairs, she pretended to be fast asleep. In reality, she didn't sleep a wink until Mike left for work the next morning.

Chapter 16

Over breakfast, Christina considered her limited options. Ordinarily, when she was sad and upset, she called her father. This was not a possibility in this situation. Nor, she thought, did she want to discuss this with Marlene. Given the way her friend felt about Mike, she would probably take his side against her. She sighed in sad resignation and poured herself another cup of coffee. She had never felt so alone in her life. What did other women do when this happened? She stared into space and fantasized herself shooting Mike, no, shooting Judy, she corrected herself quickly. Easier to get away with, and besides, she was too young to be a widow. Suddenly, she remembered her father's suggestion that she have Mike investigated. Perfect! She went to the study and pulled out the phone book. Turning to Private Investigator in the Yellow Pages, she was overwhelmed by the number of listings. Maybe she could just follow Mike herself. No, she'd never pull it off. She began reading, hoping a name would appeal to her. As she turned the page, a large color ad leaped out at her: "Police tactics in Private Investigations. Peter Wallace, ex-police sergeant". He sounds promising, she thought, and reached for the phone.

"Peter Wallace Investigations," said a female voice that sounded like someone chewing gum. "How may we be of service to you?"

"May I speak with Mr. Wallace, please?" Christina asked.

"I'll see if he's available, whom may I say is calling?" the woman on the other end chomped away, reciting words in a bored fashion.

"My name is Christina Kingsbury," she said, somewhat regally. There was a moment of silence on the other end.

"One moment, Mrs. Kingsbury." the voice said, much more clearly and with a touch of respect. Moments later, she heard a masculine voice.

"This is Peter Wallace. You are Mr. Solderburg's daughter Christina?"

"Yes."

"What may we do for you, Mrs. Kingsbury?"

"I need some discreet investigative work done." Christina was a little nervous, now that she was actually making the arrangements. "I've never done this before; do I come and see you, or do you come and see me?"

"Ordinarily, my clients come to me, Mrs. Kingsbury, but in your case I will make an exception. If you will give me your address, I will leave immediately." Before she could change her mind, Christina gave him the address. Then she hung up the phone and thought, what have I done? Her head spun in disbelief recounting the recent events.

Peter Wallace could not believe his luck. Business had not been good lately, and the bills were starting to pile up; now, this plum falls into his lap. After twenty years on the force, he knew who Paul Solderburg was, alright, and of course who his daughter was. It must be pretty serious; otherwise her father would be handling it for her. Hopefully, it was so serious she wouldn't inquire into his past too much. Of course, getting caught with a bribe didn't exactly mean you couldn't be trusted...it just meant there wasn't much you wouldn't do for money. In his business, that was usually a plus. But, an ex-police sergeant that has retired inspires more confidence than an ex-police sergeant that has been dismissed for misconduct does.

As he drove through the iron gates, Peter Wallace automatically adjusted his rates to suit his surroundings. He was clean, but tired from last night's heavy drinking, and was wearing the best suit he could find hanging in his office closet. Pulling up in front of the impressive estate, he whistled softly between his teeth, quietly estimating the fee he could charge this poor pigeon. He pushed himself out of his late-model Chevy, noticing the contrast between his car and the elegant black stretch Mercedes-Benz parked in front of the house. The cars were not the only things in sharp contrast when comparing Peter Wallace to the elegance of the estate. Peter was not only worn from heavy drinking the night before, but from heavy drinking for nearly every night for the past twenty years. While not particularly old, he appeared to be in his golden years, his cheap suit and shoes made him look the epitome of a dime-store detective. In Peter's estimation, any money spent on haircuts and manicures was liquor money misspent. This showed all too well in his appearance. However, Peter was not completely unappealing. While disheveled, he still held a glimpse of the handsome young police officer he had been twenty-five years prior, before the years of drinking, charges of misconduct, and dismissal from the force. If one looked past the surface wear and second-hand garments, the keen eyes and well-defined cheekbones and jaw were still faintly visible. He had been quite dashing in fact, years and years ago, in his handsome dress blue uniform. He rang the doorbell while checking out the house. In response to the doorbell, Steven the handy man appeared holding a screwdriver.

"Yes, Sir?" he said politely.

"I have an appointment with Mrs. Kingsbury," Peter stated firmly. Just looking at this guy made him feel old. He resolved in his head to quit smoking and get in shape, but knew it would never last.

"Your name, Sir?" Steven asked.

"Peter Wallace," he said briefly. No need to tell the household help what his profession was. Steven was wondering why Mrs. Kingsbury would want to see this rough-looking fat boy. Steven walked to a door, and knocked gently. Opening the door a crack, he announced,

"A Mr. Peter Wallace here to see you, Ma'am." Turning back

into the hallway, he motioned for Peter to go into the room, and held the door open wider. Peter stepped in, and an extremely pale Christina rose from a couch to meet him.

"I hope you don't mind meeting in the library, Mr. Wallace," she said. "It's the most private room in the house.

"Did you manage to fix that hinge yet?" she asked, turning to Steven.

"No, Ma'am, but I think I can have it done shortly." He turned and walked back across the hall. Christina did not close the door until she saw him bending to his task again. As soon as she had, however, he quietly left the hall, stepping out the front door and walking around the house to the library window. He knew it would be open a crack behind the curtains, and he could hear what was being said. Inside the library, Christina was offering Peter coffee. He would have liked something stronger, perhaps a nice double-malt Scotch, he mused, but he accepted the coffee.

"Thank you, Mrs. Kingsbury. Now, how can my firm be of service?" He figured if he made the company sound larger, she was less likely to question the fee.

"I have good reason to believe that my husband is having an affair. I want him followed for a few days – maybe a week – and photographed. How much would you charge for something like that?"

"Our fee is $500 per day, plus unexpected expenses. We usually ask for a day in advance, but since this is a sudden decision on your part..." He made it sound like a question, and Christina nodded in agreement. "I'll make an exception. But payment in full is due on delivery. For obvious reasons, we don't like to send out invoices."

"What would be considered an unexpected expense?" she asked with a puzzled look. Peter grimaced, so much for no questions.

"For example, following your husband around town may involve eating in restaurants, parking fees, that sort of thing is normal. If I follow him to the airport and he hops on a plane to

Nantucket, you'd be expected to cover my ticket over and above the daily fee."

"I see," Christina nodded again. "That will be fine, I want all the details on what he does, where he goes and with whom he meets photographed. There must be no question that I am the wronged party. I need photographs to provide indisputable proof. I would also prefer that as few people know about this as possible. I don't suppose you are available to work on the case personally?"

"I would be happy to handle this case personally, Mrs. Kingsbury. In fact, I'll keep the file sealed." He glanced at his watch. "Why don't you tell me a few things about your husband, where he works, his favorite restaurants, that sort of thing. A photograph or two would also be extremely helpful." Christina rose and walked over to the desk, passing the window where Steven ducked down and flattened himself against the wall. He had heard enough anyway. He carefully moved back around to the front door and let himself in. Christina pulled a picture out of a drawer and handed it to Peter.

"This was taken on New Year's Eve, it's the most recent picture I have."

"Nice looking guy," Peter commented. Christina thought to herself that that was why she was hiring him to do this investigation "What does he do?" As Christina gave him the information he needed, he jotted notes, then looked at his calendar. "Today is Friday. Suppose I give you a call next Thursday and let you know if I have anything?"

"That will be fine." She handed him one of her cards, and walked with him to the door of the library. As she opened it, Steven was putting tools away across the hall.

"Thank you, Mr. Wallace, I look forward to speaking with you again." She started to walk him to the front door, then noticed that Steven was already there and was holding it open. Peter shook her hand, and left, barely glancing at Steven. He was again whistling through his teeth as he reached his car. This case was going to be a snap! He went back to his office for a celebratory drink, then out to dinner. He could splurge for now, looking forward to a big fat check in a week!

Chapter 17

As Mike eased the Porsche out of the driveway, Peter followed at a safe distance, careful not to be spotted. When Mike failed to take the turn that would take him to the office, Peter almost lost him. He recovered just in time to turn a corner and see Mike pull into a restaurant parking lot. Parking on the street, he watched Mike enter the restaurant. Stealthily, he located a spot from which he could see the table where Mike was seated across from a lovely young woman. Before he could even position himself to get pictures, Mike moved his chair so that he was seated next to her, both faces visible to the camera. What a break! Peter snapped several pictures as they ate, talked, and laughed together. As Mike rose to help her with her coat, Peter zoomed in to catch a close-up of him kissing the back of her neck, in a very telling, all too familiar manner. That's a winner! thought Peter. A picture certainly is worth a thousand words, probably a thousand bucks too, the greedy man cheerfully considered.

Over the next two days, he followed them to lunch, a movie and even a motel on the edge of town. Mrs. Kingsbury was going to get her money's worth and most of it would be pure gravy, this was hardly costing him a cent! Christina, meanwhile, was beginning to have her doubts; Mike had been home every night this week in time for dinner. Wednesday evening, he had even surprised her with hard to get tickets to a popular Broadway show. Had she blown this all out of proportion? Or, she could almost hear her father saying, is that what he wants you to think? She shook her head, so wanting to believe the best, but fearing the worst. She would wait until she heard from her private detective.

Christina was in the garden pruning her mother's rose bushes, carefully practicing the rules of proper horticulture as her loving mother had instructed her. She was thinking of her mother when the phone rang, returning her to the present.

"Mr. Peter Wallace on the phone, would you like to take it out here?" Steven announced from the back door

"No, Steven, I'll come in," she answered, trying her best not to sound too anxious. If the news was bad, she did not want it spoiling her enjoyment of the garden. She had come to rely upon the garden for asylum, and dare not risk that, now more that ever. Going into the library and closing the door, she picked up the phone receiver.

"I have it, thank you," she stated, and waited until she was certain that she heard Steven hang up.

"Mr. Wallace, do you have something for me?" she asked, afraid to hear his response.

"Yes, Mrs. Kingsbury, I do. Would you like me to come over now, or is there a better time?"

"I'm not dressed for company, can you give me an hour," she lied, not even sure why she was stalling. The news wouldn't change by keeping him waiting.

"Certainly, I'll see you at eleven-thirty." As she hung up the phone, she wondered what she was going to do for the next hour. It would have been better to get it over with, wouldn't it? Her mind raced as she struggled internally over the right thing to do. Was it right to call the detective? What now? Oh, how she wished her father was here to give her advice. Restlessly, she paced the room, stopping once to call to Nancy, and ask her to serve coffee and muffins promptly at eleven-thirty-two a.m. in the library. Finally, the doorbell rang; Steven showed Peter into the library and withdrew silently. Christina served him coffee, then sat down.

"Well? Was I right?" she nervously asked.

"I'm afraid so, Mrs. Kingsbury," Peter said grimly. "He spent very little time at the office in the past three days." He handed her the pictures and sat back to watch her face react to his findings and the photos, exactly as she requested. As she looked through them, she took extremely careful note of the date/time stamp on the photos, long lunches, afternoon meetings. Now she understood. Suddenly, she stopped and flipped back through them. She focused on the close-up of Mike kissing the woman's neck and instantly went even paler, nearly the shade of one of her beloved white roses. Peter started to wonder if she might not faint. Those earrings! She couldn't believe what she was seeing. They were identical to the ones he bought her for her birthday. The ones she had lost and he had 'found' by buying her new ones. In a flash she saw the whole scenario perfectly and for the first time, clearly. Mike had taken her earrings and given them to this, this... person! He had probably hoped he could replace them before she noticed they were missing. When had they disappeared? She thought back. Halloween. The groundbreaking ceremony he didn't need her to attend! It all fit into place, the timing, her unneeded appearance and her missing earrings. This had been going on for six months!

"Do you know who this woman is?" she asked through teeth clenched in rage.

"No, Ma'am, but I can find out if you'd like to keep me on the case."

"No," she said, and then gasped, "Oh! I forgot about your money, I don't want to write a check. I will go to the bank and get cash, do you mind coming back tomorrow?" Peter hesitated. He didn't like leaving the pictures without collecting the money, but she was too upset to press the point any further. Agreeing to return in the morning, he left the house.

In the library, Christina sat down and burst into tears. What was she going to do? How could he do this to her, when they had been so much in love? Nancy knocked on the door and asked when she wanted lunch served.

"I'm not feeling well, Nancy, I'm going to go up and lie down." She went up to her room, still carrying the pictures. One more glance at the close-up, and then she tossed them on her dressing table, fell onto the bed and wept. Christina cried for hours, no longer aware of time.

Downstairs, Steven and Nancy were comparing notes. They were going to have something to report when Christina's father returned from his trip! Mike came home at six that evening.

"Honey, I'm home!" he called out gaily. There was no answer.

"Is Christina in the garden?" he asked Nancy as she came out of the kitchen.

"No, Sir, Madame was not feeling well at lunch time, and went upstairs to lie down." Mike went up to the bedroom, and gently knocked on the door.

"Christina, Honey?" He opened the door to see her lying on the bed. "How are you feeling, Baby?"

"Feeling?" Christina rolled over and sat up, her eyes red and puffy from crying. "I'll tell you how I'm feeling, you sorry son of a..." She threw herself off the bed and marched over to the dressing table. She picked up the stack of pictures and the earring box.

"I'm feeling like the biggest fool on earth! Remember these?" She shoved the box in his face. "The earrings I 'lost' in the drawer? I knew they were replacements, but I thought it was because you couldn't stand to see me upset over losing them, but now I know better." She switched hands, and thrust the pictures at him. The close-up from the restaurant was still on top.

"Tell me this isn't Judy. Tell me those aren't the earrings you bought me for my birthday in HER ears! That you didn't take them off my dressing table and give them to your... your...mistress!" She was getting close to losing control. Mike simply stood still in shock.

"How... where did you get those pictures?" he stammered, he had no forewarning, this was completely unexpected.

"I finally followed my father's good advice and had you investigated. Would you like to see the rest of them?" She began violently flipping the pictures in his face, but he turned away.

"Look, Honey, she doesn't mean anything," he began.

"Oh, really?" Christina stormed angrily around the room.

"You gave my earrings to someone who doesn't mean anything? Is that supposed to make me feel better? Those earrings disappeared six months ago, Mike. This week, you took her to breakfast, lunch, a movie and A MOTEL!" At this, Mike jumped visibly.

"Yes, I have pictures of that, too! I want you and your belongings out of my house NOW!" she commanded.

"Now? Where would I go? Honey, we can talk about this..." Mike pleaded. "This is our home." She appeared to be serious, and he suddenly realized what he had put in jeopardy by his indiscretion.

"Go to Judy. Go sleep in your office. I don't care, just get out!" She thrust the pictures at his chest, and he instinctively grabbed them. She marched over and flung the door open.

"Steven," she yelled, "bring the car around immediately. You will be driving Mr. Kingsbury wherever he wishes to go, but you will NOT be bringing him back!" With that, she slammed the door, stalked over to Mike's closet and began throwing his clothes on the bed.

"Why do I need Steven?" he unwisely reminded her, "I can just take the Porsche." He absent-mindedly put the pictures in his pocket, and walked toward her.

"Oh, no, you won't," she insisted. "That car was a gift from MY father, and it is still in MY name! This is MY house, and I want you out of it." Christina was practically screaming now.

"Honey," he reached for her, trying in vain to calm her down, "you can't throw out an entire marriage for one little indiscretion." In response to his pleading, she pulled his suitcase down from the closet shelf and threw it at him. He finally realized she wasn't going to listen, and began putting some clothes in it. Maybe he could reason with her after she calmed down a bit. He went downstairs and handed the case to Steven, who accompanied him silently outside to the car.

"Where to, Sir?" he asked, putting the bag in the trunk.

"Just head for the city, Steven, I have to think." He sat

morosely in the back seat trying to figure out what he was going to do. Slumping down, he shoved his hands in his pockets. As he did so, he felt the pictures that Christina had shoved at him in her rage. I bet she didn't mean to do this, he thought.

"Did Mrs. Kingsbury have any visitors today?" Mike asked, sitting up in his seat expectantly. Steven looked in the rear view mirror and seemed unsure whether to answer.

"Yeah, a Mr. Peter Wallace. He didn't tell me his business." That at least was true, he justified to himself. After all, it was not Mr. Kingsbury that paid his salary. He owed the man no loyalty.

"I see," said Mike thoughtfully, he was surprised he was able to obtain that much information from the usually contrary chauffeur.

"Drop me at the Hilton, will you?" He slumped in the seat again, but this time it was merely to contemplate his next move. There could be a way out of this yet. His mind began to race; he could find the way out or wait for Christina to cool down.

Once he had unpacked and called room service, he glanced at his watch. Eight-thirty, probably too late to catch Mr. Wallace in his office, but just in case, he'd look him up. Grabbing the phone book, he opened the Yellow Pages to the right page, unknowingly mimicking Christina's actions of last Friday. Finding the ad, he smiled to see an after hours number listed. He picked up the phone and dialed.

"Peter Wallace," came a tired-sounding voice.

"Mr. Wallace?" Mike did his best to sound flustered, like some pathetic soul in need, he calculated.

"I'm sorry to bother you after hours, but I have a problem. It's kind of an emergency, will you meet me at your office?"

"As a matter of fact, I'm at my office. I was just about to leave, how far away are you?" Peter sounded even more tired as he asked this.

"I can be there in five or six minutes," Mike said as he looked up the detective's address.

"OK, I'll wait," said Peter, and hung up the phone. Gulping down the last of his dinner wine, Mike called downstairs for a cab. Giving the driver the address, he leaned back and organized his thoughts, ignoring the taxi driver's look that said: 'What on earth could someone like you be doing in a neighborhood like this.'

Chapter 18

Arriving at the building, he carefully checked the address then paid the cab and entered the building. After reading the directory, he punched the elevator button for the fourth floor. Still rehearsing in his head the upcoming drama, he left the elevator to locate Mr. Wallace's office. As Mike stepped cautiously through the door, Peter walked out of an inner office. The private investigator stopped suddenly as he recognized the person he had so recently photographed.

"I should have asked your name over the phone. I can't help you, Mr. Kingsbury, I could have saved you a trip downtown."

"I would have come anyway," stated Mike flatly. He reached into his pocket and pulled out the pictures. "How many copies of these did you make for my wife?" Peter tried to refrain from showing surprise.

"I can't give you any information about your wife's case, it's against client confidentiality." Hoping that his alarm did not register on his face, he wondered why in the world Christina had given him those pictures. Would she still pay him, or try to get out of it?

"Confidentiality my eye. You aren't a lawyer, Wallace," Mike said angrily. "I've been thrown out of the house, and my wife is going to file for divorce. I have a right to know if she has this evidence to use in court."

"I only gave her one copy, but she won't need them anyway, there are plenty of witnesses to your assignations with the lady." Peter was getting angry now, too. He may not be a lawyer, but he didn't need a snot-nosed pretty boy with a rich wife telling him what to do.

"Money talks, Wallace. Those witnesses will be hard to find. Speaking of which, how much did she pay you to spy on me?"

"Now, that's something I won't tell you," replied Peter, his voice rising with his temper. "Our business is finished." He made a move as if to walk Mike to the door, but Mike didn't budge.

"Not quite," he said belligerently. "I'll pay you five thousand dollars for the negatives," he added, fanning the private eye with the photos as he waved them directly under Peter's nose.

"I don't think so. If anyone gets these, it will be your wife." Despite his chivalrous comment, Peter was already mentally preparing a list of possibilities for a little additional cash. It had been a slow year...real slow.

"Look, you couldn't possibly have made this much working for her, ten thousand and that's my final offer. What have you got to lose?" Peter considered his options. There was a possibility he might not get paid at all for this job, why not take the easy money?

"Alright," he said, "but it has to be cash. You'll have to come back tomorrow." Peter reminded himself that 'all is fair in love and war', besides, ten thousand dollars was more money than he would seen in one place for a year.

"As soon as the bank opens." Mike strode from the dingy office triumphantly. After Mike left, Peter stood and thought for a moment. He remembered the pain in Christina's beautiful, yet sad, big brown eyes. The pictures, one in particular seemed to be the source of this acute pain. What was it about that picture in particular? Why had she given them to him? Or had he taken them by force? Slowly, he went to a file drawer and pulled out an envelope marked "Kingsbury". He locked his office door and headed into his darkroom.

"Cancel any appointments or meetings I have for today." Mike's secretary was professional enough not to say anything, but her eyes widened slightly in surprise. He didn't give her the opportunity to respond as he quickly left the office and headed for the elevator in his signature stride.

Walking into the bank, he walked up and handed the teller a check made out to 'cash' for fifteen thousand dollars on their joint account.

"How would you like that, Mr. Kingsbury?" asked the teller respectfully. "Would large bills be alright?"

"I'll need five thousand of it in nothing larger than hundreds." Mike answered. He waited impatiently while the teller called the bank manager, and they retrieved his money from the vault. Once the transaction was complete, he hailed a cab and went straight to Peter's office.

Mike looked forward to the day when he would not have to return to this neighborhood. Looking out the window he saw what appeared to be a drug deal gone bad. He leaned against the seat in the cab, closed his eyes, and let his mind drift to thoughts of happier days. Peter was standing at his secretary's desk when Mike walked in.

"Mr. Kingsbury, come right in," he said as he led the way into his own office.

"I've got the money, where are my negatives?" Mike demanded. "I have things to do."

"Relax, Kingsbury, they're right here." Peter picked up the envelope of negatives and held out his hand for the money. "I hope you didn't short me. I do know where you work." He chuckled, only half joking.

"It's all there, count it if you want." Mike taunted the investigator, as he looked through the pictures, making sure none were held back. All he needed was a blackmailing private eye.

"You guarantee that you only made my wife one copy of these?"

"Absolutely," Peter said. He was glad Mike had asked the question that way, after all, the copy he had made last night was for his own files.

"Good," said Mike, reaching into his pocket and taking out a gold cigarette lighter. Setting the corner of the envelope ablaze, he held it over the metal wastebasket by Peter's desk. Just before it threatened to burn his fingers, he dropped it in.

"That takes care of that," he declared, as he took one last look around the office.

Chapter 19

New York City, New York
May 16, 1992

At the Kingsbury house, Christina was exhausted. She hadn't slept all night, tossing and turning and wondering if she had done the right thing. Her father was going to be impossible, saying 'I told you so'. She wished he wasn't out of town, she really needed to talk to him. She crawled out of bed to get ready for the day. As she sat at her dressing table fixing her hair, she suddenly missed the packet of pictures. In her mind's eye, she saw herself shoving them at Mike. He must have kept them! Swiftly, her thoughts spurred on by growing anger, she calculated that she owed Peter Wallace four thousand dollars; she would pay him an extra thousand for another copy of the pictures. Maybe he would even give her the negatives. She wasn't sure how these things worked. Leaving the bedroom, she called to Steven and informed him that he would be driving her to the bank. Once there, she coincidentally approached the same teller Mike had used earlier, handing him a check made out to 'cash' for five-thousand dollars.

"Must be your anniversary or something, huh?" he said with a wink.

"I beg your pardon," Christina said, puzzled.

"Well," he stated, leaning forward in a conspiratorial manner, "Mr. Kingsbury was in here just after we opened the bank, and he cashed a rather large check..." his voice trailed off as he saw the look of extreme distress on Christina's face.

"How much," she asked tightly, "did he ask for?"

When the teller hesitated, she asked to see the manager. When the manager arrived at the window, Christina reminded him in a carefully controlled voice that not only was she a long-time customer of this bank, but so was her father. She asked him how unhappy he would be if both of them changed banks.

"I don't understand," the manager said. "Is there a problem?"

"I want to know exactly how much my husband withdrew from the account this morning," she repeated. The manager punched a few buttons on the computer.

"I show a check cashed this morning for fifteen-thousand dollars." Christina finished cashing her check, and stumbled numbly from the bank in a state of shock. Why would Mike need that kind of money, and in cash? Was he spending it on a love-nest with Judy? Was he being blackmailed? Had he hired some high-priced lawyer to file for divorce first? The more she thought about it, the angrier she became.

Arriving home, she called Peter.

"I have your money, plus an extra thousand," she told him. "I'm afraid I foolishly allowed my husband to walk away with the pictures you brought me, and I'll need new copies, or maybe I could buy the negatives?" There was an uncomfortable silence on the other end of the line.

"I'm afraid the negatives have been burned, Mrs. Kingsbury. As I told you before, to keep it discreet, I do this with all my important clients. I burn all my documents," Peter lied. "And I don't have any copies."

"Oh," she said in a small voice. "Well, come and get the money I owe you anyway."

"I'll be there in about an hour," he stated. "I'm waiting for a phone call." After she hung up, Christina thought over her options. If only her father was home! He could help her organize her thoughts. What kind of weapons could Mike use against her, he was the one that was wrong, wasn't he? Suddenly, she had a thought. Going to the door of the library, she called for Steven.

"When you drove Mr. Kingsbury away last night, where did you take him?"

"To the Hilton, Ma'am," Steven said respectfully. "He wasn't sure at first, but then..." he hesitated.

"Then what?" Christina prompted.

"After I mentioned Mr. Wallace's name, he..."

"You what?!" Christina yelled. She seemed almost ready to strike him. "Whatever possessed you to do that?"

"Well, he asked if there had been any visitors," Steven was more hesitant in his replies now.

"And you forgot exactly who it is that pays your salary, and told him all about Mr. Wallace?" Christina was angry, but she seemed to make an effort to control her voice.

"All he has to do is look in the phone book, and he'll know everything! I should fire you on the spot!"

"I'm sorry, Mrs. Kingsbury, I didn't mean to cause any trouble." Steven apologized as humbly as he could, hoping that it looked sincere. He couldn't lose this job; he had become too used to the generous salary. Besides, getting fired by the Solderburg-Kingsbury family would make it very difficult to find work someplace else. Christina drew a deep breath. She had to pull herself together; she was seeing enemies around every corner.

"No, of course you didn't," she conceded. "Just remember in the future that what goes on in this household should remain private, and Mr. Kingsbury is no longer to be considered a member of this household." Almost unconsciously, she had slipped back into the regal tone of voice her parents always used with their servants.

"Yes, Ma'am," Steven said, feeling properly chastised. Just then the doorbell rang.

"No, I'll get it," said Christina hurriedly. She dismissed Steven with a wave towards the back of the house, and he vanished into the kitchen; it was his lunchtime anyway. Christina opened the door, and stepped out onto the porch, not allowing Peter into the house.

"How much of the fifteen thousand did it take for you to burn those negatives?" she demanded of him, catching him completely off guard.

"What?" Peter was taken aback. "What do you mean?" He could see that she was too angry to even attempt a bluff, so he tried a different tactic.

"Now, Mrs. Kingsbury, why don't you calm down a minute."

"Calm down? I hired you to get evidence on my husband, and you sell him the very evidence I need! He has the pictures, you are saying that you've burned the negatives, I have nothing! Which is exactly what I should pay you!"

"You hired me to follow your husband and find out if he was having an affair; I did that. I am not the one who gave him the pictures; you did that. What I did with the negatives doesn't matter, the case should have been closed. It would have been if you had paid me on delivery like you agreed. You owe me four-thousand dollars, and that's all there is to it!" he argued.

"Well, I don't agree! You don't get a dime until I have a copy of those pictures!" Almost too fast for him, she was inside the front door and starting to slam it; he was barely able to stop it with his hand.

"Mrs. Kingsbury, you don't realize who you are messing with. I WILL get my money from you, one way or another." he threatened.

Letting go of the door so fast that she almost slammed her own hand in it, he stomped down the steps to his car. Christina watched him drive away and tried to breathe a sigh of relief, as his car disappeared around the curve, but she was trembling. Did he mean it? Would he really hurt her for the money? Oh, why didn't her father come home! Then she remembered something; Mike still had access to their bank account. He could take everything. She had to act fast! Calling to Steven, she went upstairs and grabbed an empty suitcase from her closet. Running back down the stairs, she almost careened into Steven. Recovering, she told him to bring the car around.

When they arrived at the bank, she walked up to the same teller and demanded to see the manager.

"What can we do for you, Mrs. Kingsbury?" the Manager asked as he approached her.

"I want to close my account," she stated flatly. The man paled visibly.

"It's not about what happened this morning, and nothing against you or your staff, I just want to make sure my husband can't take out any more than he already has," she reasoned.

"Why don't we step into my office, where we can work everything out in private," he suggested. As they sat down at the desk, he punched up the account on his computer.

"After the two withdrawals today, you still have over a hundred and twenty-five thousand dollars in this account alone. Are you sure you wouldn't just like to open a savings account in your own name?" the manager asked hopefully.

"No, that would just complicate things," Christina chewed on her lower lip. "If he decides to fight the divorce, he could freeze my assets. My best friend's husband is a lawyer, and he talked about that once. I want it out of his reach. I have a large safe at home and I can get the combination changed. My father will advise me what else to do when he comes home tomorrow."

"Very well," said the manager, and called for a teller to process the closure. When Christina and Steven left the bank, he was carrying the bag now uncomfortably heavy with the weight of Christina's money. He started to put it in the trunk automatically, but Christina stopped him and said she didn't want it out of her sight. They drove straight home, with the suitcase resting heavily on the seat next to Christina. When they arrived, Steven carried the bag upstairs and put it on her dressing table bench. After dismissing Steven, Christina closed and locked the door. Opening the safe, she began to stack the money inside. She also grabbed her credit cards and placed them next to the necklace, and her other jewelry. No use taking chances, she thought. When the suitcase was empty, she closed the safe, twirled the knob, and put the suitcase back in the closet. Finally, with her mind at ease, she went down to lunch.

Mike drove through the front gates, in a rented car, to see if he could speak with Christina. Steven was out front, polishing the front fender of the limo. Mike paused briefly, reminiscing over the night of Christina's birthday. Steven straightened up and moved toward Mike, stopping him from coming any closer to the house.

"Is Mrs. Kingsbury at home?" asked Mike, not backing away, but not pushing himself past Steven either. The handyman had more muscles than he had ever even thought about having.

"Yes, Sir," Steven answered, slightly less than respectfully. "But I have strict orders not to let you enter. In fact, if you don't leave the property at once, I'll have to notify the authorities. I'm not going to lose my job over this," he warned.

"Ok, ok, I'm going," Mike retreated to the car. "At least tell her I came by."

When there was no answer from Steven, he wrenched the car door open and flung himself into the seat. Driving away, he decided he needed a little something to get him through the long night ahead, but he certainly didn't want to hang out in some bar. Driving to the liquor store, he went in and selected a bottle of whiskey. At the cash register, he handed the clerk the debit card for their joint bank account.

"I'm sorry, Sir, this will not go through," she told him. "The machine says the card is denied."

"That bitch!" Mike shouted, exploding in anger. "I can't believe she would go this far. She's going to be sorry for this!" The manager came hurrying from the back room to see who was creating all the ruckus. At his appearance, Mike realized what a scene he was causing, and calmed down a fraction. He apologized to both of them, aware of the importance of appearances at a time like this, and paid by cash for the whiskey and left the store, muttering under his breath.

By nine-thirty, Christina was convinced that Mike would not come back that night, and told Steven to go ahead and go home;

she and Nancy would be fine. Just as a precaution, she told him to double-check that the gates closed properly after he drove out. Pouring herself a cup of coffee, she went into the parlor to try to relax. As she sat down, the phone rang, causing her to almost drop the cup. Taking a deep breath and a small drink of the steaming hot coffee, she picked up the phone. Her father's voice greeting her from the other end of the phone quickly brought tears to her eyes; she was so glad to hear it.

"Daddy!" she exclaimed "I didn't expect you until tomorrow afternoon! I'm so glad you're back. Can you come over for breakfast tomorrow? I really need to talk to you." Her voice became thick with emotion, starting and stopping between sobs, two small trails of tears running down her cheeks. Paul grew concerned as he listened to her sobbing.

"What's wrong, Honey?" her father said gently. "Is it Mike? What's he done now?"

"Yes, daddy," she hiccupped. "I suspected he was having an affair, so I had him investigated. I hired a Mr. Peter Wallace, have you heard of him?" Paul said something under his breath.

"Yes, I've heard of him, and I wish I had been here to stop you. Any other investigator would have been better. But it's too late now, what did he find out?" he asked, trying to sound calm.

"He took pictures, Daddy." The tears were flowing. "Mike has been seeing this woman for six months! He takes her to shows and movies and motels and gives her expensive presents..." She took a deep breath, trying to calm herself. "Anyway, I threw him out and closed the bank account. He tried to come back and see me tonight, but Steven stopped him from coming in. I really need your advice," she pleaded.

"Well, I'll give you a little now. Make sure the gates are closed and all the windows and doors are locked. Be very sure to set the security alarm tonight. Are you sure you don't want me to come over immediately?"

"No, Daddy, you get some sleep. I know traveling tires you out. Now that I know you are home, I will sleep better," she lied.

"Just come over for breakfast about eight-thirty, ok?" They agreed to meet in the morning and said goodnight.

"I am so glad you're home, Daddy. I love you," Christina added before hanging up. Paul was surprised by his daughter's display of affection

"Me too baby, me too," and hung up the phone. This was one of those rare times that he felt helpless, despite all of his money and connections. Oh how he wished he'd been wrong about Mike.

Christina checked the French doors leading to the garden. Seeing they were locked, she drew the curtains over them. Then she went out into the hallway and checked the front door; it was locked as well. Nancy was headed to her room, so Christina called to her to be double sure the alarm was set before she went upstairs to her room. Lying in the king-size bed alone, she wondered anew if she had done the right thing. She knew her father would be able to help her make sense of it all in the morning, and that he would know just what should be done next. Knowing that she had done all she could for the time being, she closed her eyes. She might as well try to get a good night's sleep.

Chapter 20

New York City, New York
May 17, 1992

Nancy tapped on the door of the master bedroom in passing.

"Mrs. Kingsbury," she called out. "Coffee's ready, your father called to say he'll be here in fifteen minutes." She continued down the hall to open the large draperies over the end window, letting the morning light fill the hallway. Turning around, she frowned to see that the door was still closed. In fact, there was no sign that Christina had responded at all. She walked back to the bedroom door, and knocked a little louder.

"Mrs. Kingsbury? Did you hear me?" This was unlike Christina, she thought. She opened the door far enough to see that the bed was mussed and empty; no sign of Christina. She entered the room, assuming that Christina was in the bathroom, but stopped cold in her tracks when she saw the fireplace. With terror and disbelief she saw Christina lying on the floor with a puddle of blood at her head. Stepping around the end of the bed, Nancy crouched down closer to see if Christina was still breathing. Finding no sign of life, she concluded that she must be dead. Nancy ran from the room, calling for Steven at the top of her voice. Steven came running from the kitchen, hearing the terror in her voice, he took a hold of her as she reached the bottom of the stairs.

"What? What is it?" He demanded. He shook her slightly to stop her sobs so he could understand her.

"Mrs. Kingsbury is dead," she managed to gasp out. "She's fallen and hit her head on the mantel. What are we going to do?"

"Are you sure?" he started up the stairs, but Nancy grabbed his arm.

"She's lying on the floor, there's blood..." Seeing that she was close to hysteria again, Steven came back down and took her by the shoulders again. He started to talk to her, interrupted almost immediately by the doorbell. Hoping it was Mr. Solderburg, he let go of Nancy, and went to open the front door. Seeing Christina's father, Nancy burst into tears once again.

"Nancy! What on earth?" He, too, grabbed her shoulders.

"Is it Christina? Is she alright?" he demanded. As she violently shook her head, he released her and ran up the stairs. Bursting into the bedroom, he spotted her body and knelt down beside it. Choking back his own tears, he took a look around to see if he could see any evidence of foul play. Besides the fact that her eyes were still open and staring, an indication of violent trauma, he noticed that her hand was clenched, and spotted something in it. This was no accident; someone had murdered his only child! A rage unlike any other began to take hold of him. He could see only retribution at his hand. He would see that whoever it was paid for this crime, if it took all his resources. He noticed the safe was opened half way and found that it was empty. He retreated from the room, closing the door, leaving the scene as he had found it. Making his way down the stairs, his steps mechanical, he choked back his tears of grief. He couldn't help but remember back to when Christina was a child, how he'd loved and cherished his little girl, now she was gone forever. The pealing of the doorbell suddenly returned him to the present. It was Marlene Endicott.

"Marlene," Paul said, realizing that he would have to break the news to Christina's best friend that she was dead. He took Marlene by the arm and steered her into the library.

"You look like something is wrong, what is it?" Marlene inquired. Paul was quiet.

"I just came up on a whim." Marlene said. "I checked into the Hilton last night and thought I'd surprise Christina this morning. Is she up yet?" Paul motioned for Marlene to sit on a sofa in the library and hesitantly, he told Marlene what he had just discovered upstairs.

"No! I don't believe it!" Marlene jumped up as if to run upstairs to the bedroom, but Paul stopped her.

"I've seen her, Marlene, she's gone. She was robbed, and probably murdered."

"Where was Mike?" she sobbed, tears rolling unchecked down her face. "Is he alright?" Paul gritted his teeth. How could she worry about Mike? He was the most likely suspect, wasn't he? And Christina was her best friend! Still, his voice was gentle when he answered.

"She and Mike were separated, Marlene, he wasn't staying in this house last night." As she gave into her tears, he eased her back down onto the sofa, and let her cry it out. Calling to Nancy, Paul asked her to bring Marlene some strong tea, and then went to the phone on the table to call the police. It was then he realized that he too was in shock, a deep shock from losing his only beloved child. He allowed himself to weep now, mourning her loss. Mixed with his tears of sorrow were the bitter tears of anger as he vowed, once again, to never rest until the person responsible for this unspeakable, horrible act paid, and paid dearly indeed.

The police had finished their investigation of the crime scene, and Christina's body was being taken away to the morgue in the grim vehicle labeled, 'State of New York Coroner'. When they had arrived, the police had firmly instructed Paul not to let anyone leave the house, or touch anything, so he and Marlene were in the parlor, neither of them saying anything. Steven and Nancy had gone to the kitchen. Nancy was trying to fix something for them, although her sobs still shook her from time to time. Steven was sitting at the kitchen table having coffee, so that he could get back to his chores when the police were finished questioning him. Both of them were wondering what the future held for them, now that the woman they worked for was gone. Would Mr. Solderburg find them another position, or would they be left on their own? It was certain they would not be kept on here, if Mike Kingsbury retained the house.

Steven and Nancy both jumped as an officer entered.

"Sorry," he said, "I didn't mean to startle you. We need to talk to each of you separately, is there somewhere else we can go?"

"You'll want Nancy first, she found her." Steven rose from the table. "I'll just go out back and clean out the garage. Call out the back door when you're ready for me," he suggested.

"Actually, my partner will talk to you," the officer said, "I'll send him out when he's ready." Steven nodded and went out the back door. The officer smiled at Nancy and asked her to have a seat at the table. He had conducted many such interviews and had a particularly soothing tone.

"Now, then, Nancy, you found the body?" he asked as gently as he could. He could tell she had obviously been crying.

"Yes, sir," she sniffled. "I went in to tell her that her father was on his way and that her coffee was getting cold. She was just lying there, blood all over the place, staring out with those big brown eyes." She shuddered. "It ain't natural to die with your eyes open, must have been awful sudden. Fell and hit her head, or something, did she?" She looked at him hopefully, but he shook his head.

"I'm sorry, but I'm asking the questions here. I need to ask you about what you did last evening. When did you retire for the night?"

"Shortly after Steven left, about nine-thirty. Wait, I think it was later than that, because I was just going in to ask Mrs. Kingsbury if she needed anything else when the phone rang. It was her father, home a day early. I went back to the kitchen so as not to overhear, and waited for her to hang up."

"If you couldn't hear, how would you know she hung up?" the detective asked.

"There's a light on the phone that tells if the phone is in use. It's there so that someone doesn't accidentally pick up the extension while Mr. Kingsbury is on a business call. I sat right here, right in this very spot in fact, at the table and waited, I noticed that the time on the phone said that it was about nine forty-five, then I went out. She was coming out of the room, and asked me to make sure the alarm was set and the doors and windows locked. It was the second night she spent alone with no man in the house, and I think she was getting a little nervous." Nancy's eyes widened and she looked at the officer in shock and recognition of what had transpired.

"You're surely not telling me she was murdered! Right here in this house, with me asleep in the basement?" She looked at the officer in disbelief. "Oh! I should have been more careful. Oh poor Christina." She began moaning and rocking back and forth on the chair.

"My poor Christina!" The officer was visibly shaken by her reaction and unsure how to proceed. He breathed a sigh of relief when a doctor entered the kitchen.

"If you are through questioning Mrs. Clapper, I'd like to take a look at her," the doctor said, in a tone that suggested that the questioning should cease soon. Gratefully, the officer accepted the broad hint offered, leaving the doctor to take Nancy to her room where he administered a heavy sedative. The shock of the morning's event was just too much for the woman, the doctor included in his medical dictation later that day. The police officer had left the kitchen in search of Paul Solderburg. As the officer entered the parlor, he noted the lovely young lady on the sofa. He also spotted Paul and turned to him with a questioning look on his face.

"Is this young lady a member of the household?" he asked.

"No," Marlene looked up at him; her eyes were still full of tears. "I came to town last night to surprise Christina. I live in Boston."

"But you've been in town since last night?" She nodded.

"I'm afraid I'm going to have to ask you where you were and what you were doing before you arrived here." His question was met with a glare of open hostility. His apologetic look did nothing to reduce Marlene's obvious resentment at being questioned. She looked at him, comprehension dawning on her face.

"You don't think I had anything to do with Christina's death, do you? I'm her best friend!" Resentment gave way to indignation, how dare he even suggest such a thing!

"Ma'am, we're dealing with a sudden death here, we have to investigate everyone connected with the victim," he said in the most reasonable voice he could manage. The officer was having trouble remaining professional; he found that despite many years on the force, he was still not immune to Marlene's breathtaking appearance.

"Oh," she said, deliberately drawing a deep breath. "Well, I took the train up from Boston yesterday evening. I checked into the Hilton right around dinnertime. I took a cab to a favorite restaurant of mine, across town. I expect the Hilton doorman will remember me, he had a devil of a time hailing a cab that time of day. I used to live here," she explained. "I moved when my husband got a new job. Anyway, after dinner I went back to the hotel and went to bed. I was tired from the trip, and I wanted to be fresh when I saw..." her voice trailed off, and she began sobbing uncontrollably, unable to finish her sentence. After sometime she was able to add, "I got here and Paul told me!"

"Mr. Solderburg," the officer said as he turned to his left. "I'm afraid I'm going to have to ask you all the same questions."

"Of course, I understand," Paul said quietly. "I arrived home yesterday evening around eight. You can ask my housekeeper if you need a more exact time. I was a day early, and she was quite flustered, having neither my bed made up nor anything ready for me to eat. I am certain she will clearly remember my arrival." He paused briefly remembering the tongue-lashing he gave his poor housekeeper.

"I called Christina last night at nine-thirty, letting her know I was home early. She asked me to come over this morning for breakfast, so here I am. As I'm sure Nancy will tell you, I called about a quarter after because I thought I would be late, but as it happens I arrived at precisely eight-thirty."

"Thank you both, I appreciate your cooperation. Now, your daughter was Mrs. Kingsbury? Where is Mr. Kingsbury?"

"He is no longer living in the house. My daughter discovered that he had been having an affair, and asked him to leave. I don't know whether that was yesterday or the day before, you'll have to ask the staff, they will remember clearly I'm sure." Paul failed to notice how white Marlene had gone while he was speaking. Her wonderful perfect Mike! The example she was constantly comparing with her Kevin. Mike had an affair! She could not believe it, was it possible? It was almost too much to comprehend! The officer thanked them both again and left the room. Unlike Paul, the officer had noticed the extreme change in Marlene. He stopped in the hall outside the library and added this observation to his thorough notes. Meanwhile, his partner had questioned Steven in the garage.

"Yes, I left the house last night at nine-thirty. That's about what time I always go home after work. Mrs. Kingsbury seemed a bit nervous, her husband had been gone for two days, and she had all that money in the house."

"She keeps a large amount of money on the premises?"

"Well, not usually, but she does now. Yesterday I drove her to the city, where she closed the bank account after she threw Mr. Kingsbury out."

"I see. Isn't it unusual for a chauffeur to live off the premises?" the officer asked while making a mental note to not forget all that cash on the premises.

"Yeah, well, I was originally hired just as the handyman. Then, Mr. Kingsbury decided he didn't want Mrs. Kingsbury to have to drive in city traffic, and I've lived in worse cities than this, so I became the chauffeur as well. I live with my mother, taking care of her, and Mr. Solderburg arranged for my mother to have a nurse during the day while I work. Mama wants me home at night. She doesn't trust anyone else while she's sleeping," he added.

"I think that about does it for now. If we want to talk to you again, may we contact you here, or elsewhere?"

"I don't know for sure. I'll have to see what Mr. Solderburg has in mind for me. It's really him I work for."

Both officers approached Paul to inquire about the money, which Steven mentioned. Paul pointed them to the safe and told them that, last night, Christina mentioned something about the money and that she had placed it in the safe. The officers noticed that the safe was open and appeared to be completely empty. They sealed the room and decided that they had enough to go on for now. As they headed toward the patrol car, they issued the customary warning to all, not to leave the city without informing the police department. The officers took Marlene's Boston address and phone number, and she assured them that she would not be leaving until after some sort of funeral or service for Christina had been held. Secretly, she was wondering how to get in touch with Mike before the police did. They were probably already on their way to his office; she decided that it was better not to interfere. Saying goodbye to Paul, she left to hail a cab and return to her hotel.

Paul, meanwhile, called Nancy and Steven into the kitchen and assured them that they would continue to work for him. He would find them something in his own household as soon as all this calmed down. They could have some time off with pay, if they wanted. Steven quickly accepted, saying that he would like that, to be able to spend some time with his mother. Nancy called her sister, living in New Jersey, and arranged to spend some time with her there. Before their departure, both staff members agreed to be available whenever he needed them. Paul then turned his attention to the task of closing the estate; he closed up the house, took one last look, and set the alarm. It was still hard to believe that Christina was gone forever.

In the privacy of his study, Paul began to grieve. He could feel each of the stages of grief as they passed through his body and discovered that of these generally accepted stages, the most frequent and prominent stage was anger. Even as he finally gave way to tears, his anger percolated, becoming more potent. He silently vowed he would find who did this and make certain that they were punished to the full extent of the law, perhaps even more, he considered.

Chapter 21

Mike looked up from his paperwork, irritated. The office was closed, the door was locked, why did they insist on knocking? All of his recent absences had made him desperately behind on several deadlines. Reluctantly tossing his pen on the desk, he stood up to go see who was so persistent. As he strained to see who was bothering him, he could only see shadows through the frosted glass. When he opened the door, the two men he saw standing outside were stereotypical police detectives, just like those whom you would see on TV, the smaller of the two men even had a broken nose. The tallest of the pair showed his badge and handled the introductions.

"I am Detective Harrison, this is my partner Detective Williams." The other man nodded at the sound of his name. "May we come in?" Puzzled, Mike opened the door wider and stepped back in an unspoken invitation. They entered the room, looking around as though they did not fully expect him to be alone.

"What's this all about, Detectives?" he asked nervously.

"Perhaps you'd better sit down, Mr. Kingsbury," the detective suggested as he wheeled over a chair and purposefully waited until Mike sat down. Detective Harrison pulled out his notebook.

"We have bad news for you. Your wife was robbed and possibly murdered late last night, Mr. Kingsbury." Both men watched Mike very closely for his reaction to the news that would be devastating to a happily married man. Without allowing time for a response from their possible suspect, they pursued the questioning.

"Sir, we need to know where you were last evening, say, after dinner." Mike just sat still and stared at them.

"Robbed? What do you mean, possibly murdered? Is she dead or has she disappeared?" Mike asked, sincerely hoping for the latter, leaving a chance for her survival.

"Last night, someone cleaned out the safe in your bedroom – former bedroom. Your wife apparently hit her head on the mantle of the fireplace, and died at the scene. We have yet to prove whether she fell or was pushed, but rest assured, Mr. Kingsbury, we will find out what happened. Now, you can talk to us here, or we can take you down to the precinct." He started to put his notebook away, indicating that he intended to do the latter, but Mike shook his head, genuinely shaken by the disturbing news. Mike rubbed his hand over his face, pausing to rub his now pulsing temples.

"Last night, I worked until about six, went to dinner at the steak house on the next block, had some drinks with a friend I ran into, went back to the hotel and slept. I arrived at work this morning around eight-thirty."

"Were you alone at the hotel, Sir?" the detective asked.

"I beg your pardon?" Mike asked, not fully understanding the implication of their question.

"Mr. Kingsbury, we were told that you no longer reside in your late wife's house because of an extra-marital affair. If you have a witness to your movements last night, it would prove helpful."

"Oh, I see. No, I wasn't with her," Mike stammered wearily. "I haven't seen her in two or three days."

"When was the last time you saw your wife alive?"

"The night she threw me out, God, was it only two nights ago? Seems like forever. Anyway, Thursday night."

"You didn't see her Friday at all?" The two detectives exchanged glances that Mike didn't like or understand.

"No, I did not!" Mike was becoming a little defensive now; he was beginning to see the direction their questions were taking. "And I didn't kill her either! We'd had a quarrel, but I had every intention of patching it up."

"The young lady's name?" The detective looked straight into Mike's eyes. "We'll need to ascertain her whereabouts as well."

"No! She is not involved in this!" Mike sounded adamant.

"Mr. Kingsbury," the detective said patiently, "It wouldn't be the first time a mistress kills a wife to gain a husband. Her name please?" Mike looked at him in shock.

"Judy Brown, she works for the city," he said, almost unconsciously. Mike's mind was spinning. He never intended for this to happen. Regret swept over him. All he could think about was poor Christina, gone.

"Thank you, Mr. Kingsbury, you've been most helpful. Oh, one more thing, the name of the hotel where you are staying?"

"The Hilton, downtown." Mike didn't understand the second look that passed between the two detectives either, but right now, he didn't care. He showed them out, then closed and locked the office door. Sitting back down at his desk, he stared uncomprehendingly into space. Christina dead? What was he going to do now? Mike picked up the phone and dialed. Sam Barber, his longtime friend and lawyer answered on the other end.

"Mike! I was just about to call you. It was just on the news, are you alright? What did they mean, 'estranged husband'?"

"Sam, can I come and talk to you?" Sam heard the unmistakable sound of fear in Mike's trembling voice.

"Of course, come on up to the house, I'll have Martha put on some coffee."

Meanwhile, the two detectives had located Judy Brown at home. Standing on the porch, they rang the doorbell, and waited. When Judy looked through the peephole, they showed their badges, and asked if they might come in and ask a few questions. She opened the door with a puzzled look on her face.

"Yes, officer, what is it?" she appeared concerned.

"It's detective, Miss Brown, and we're sorry to bother you. There's been a very serious crime committed, and we need to know where you were last night." Just then the television that Judy had on in the living room switched to a news story about

Christina's murder. Judy turned to look at the screen with wide eyes, then turned back to the detectives.

"Is that the crime you mean?" She seemed to sway on her feet, then pivoted and walked into the living room. Sitting down, she buried her face in her hands for a long moment. Finally, she raised her head and took a deep breath, and turned to face them.

"I was here last night, but there are no witnesses. I did not see Mike Kingsbury, I know that's the next question. We have not seen each other since lunch on Thursday. I was going to call his office this afternoon, to see if he was working. I guess I won't now." She gave a shaky laugh, then rubbed her hands over her face again.

"No, Ma'am, I wouldn't advise it. You say you were home last night, when did you arrive here?"

"Six o'clock, just in time for the evening news," she stated with certainty. "I always watch it while I'm fixing dinner if I'm home. I had dinner, watched a TV movie, and then went upstairs and read until about midnight. Not much of an alibi, if you're saying I need one."

"At this point, we haven't ruled out anyone, Miss Brown. Please stay where we can reach you," they advised.

"Of course." She rose to accompany them to the door. "How...I mean, what happened?"

"We're not at liberty to discuss that, Miss Brown. We don't want anyone turning in false confessions or jumping to conclusions." He looked her straight in the eye when he said this, and she blanched. After they had gone, she went back to the living room, staring unseeing at the television. As she sat there, tears began to fall, and she cried remorsefully until she fell asleep on the couch.

Chapter 22

As Mike pulled into the drive at Sam Barber's house, Sam came out the front door to meet him.

"I can't believe it!" he exclaimed. "Come inside and put your feet up, we'll talk." Sam was a big blustery man, rough and outdoorsy, practically the opposite of Mike in every way. The two of them had met in college, and somehow remained friends despite their different outlooks on life. When a client of Mike's threatened to sue over imagined fraud, he had called Sam for advice, and Sam had been his lawyer ever since. As he gratefully drank the strong, hot coffee, Mike poured out the events of the last two days.

"It's all her father's fault. He has always hated me, and he talked her into having me investigated," Mike explained.

"But, Mike, you were having an affair, you can't blame her father for that. That was your own choice." Sam was openly annoyed at Mike's inability or unwillingness to assume any responsibility for his infidelity.

"It doesn't mean I killed her!" Mike was so agitated, that he spilled his coffee and Sam jumped up to help him before it burned Mike's leg.

"No, of course not, but blaming everyone for your estrangement isn't going to help. Take responsibility for what you have done, and deny what you haven't. If you tell the truth about everything, you are more likely to be believed." Sam made the pointed statement with cause. Having known Mike for as long as he had, Sam was afraid that the truth would be hard to find in this ordeal. He cared about Mike but knew him all too well. Sighing, Mike settled down, and the two men talked all afternoon.

When Mike left, he felt a lot better; his good friend gave him a small amount of peace of mind. He was still left to deal with Christina's sudden death and was horribly racked with guilt. Mike agonized over the knowledge that he had betrayed his wife. His mind tortured him with the image of her dying, alone and heartbroken by the betrayal by her husband. He knew he would never stop regretting his actions, nor would he ever forget his beautiful brown-eyed wife, Christina. He thought about going up to the house, but instead he just went back to his hotel and sat thinking. His mind drifted to recount all the things he wished he'd done for her or said. He wished he had the chance to dance with her, just as she always wished he would.

Since the police would not release the body for burial, Paul had decided to have a memorial service for Christina as soon as possible. The memorial would be something for the public to attend. Later, he would quietly and very privately, bury her next to her mother. He knew in his heart this was how he wished to grieve the loss of his only child - privately. He had not shown his grief publicly, nor did he intend to. He would honor his daughter and her memory in solitude, away from the public eye. His heart ached; it felt like it was quite literally breaking at the thought of his loss. Quickly, as if a light was switched on, his grief gave way to anger. His resolve to make certain her husband paid for this travesty was strengthened; he knew this feeling would never be diminished.

At the memorial, Marlene was one of the first to arrive, she walked up to Paul and gave him a hug.

"I'm glad you decided to do this instead of waiting. I will have to go back to Boston soon." She didn't sound too happy about it, he noted.

"Yes, well, it's a shame Kevin couldn't get away to be with you today," was his only comment. She made a face as if to say 'I wouldn't want him to' and started to enter the chapel. As Marlene turned, she spotted Mike walking in, and so did Paul, who strode angrily towards him, his fury plainly written on his face.

"You are the reason that my daughter's dead," he snarled, "and I'm going to see that you pay!" Turning on his heel he stormed into the chapel; he couldn't help but notice that Marlene lingered outside to talk to Mike.

"Are you alright?" she asked gently, laying a hand on his arm, then she immediately shook her head. "What a stupid thing to say, of course you're not alright. Mike, if there's anything I can do, just let me know."

"Thanks, Marlene. It's nice to know there's someone on my side." He took her elbow and escorted her inside.

Marlene remained at Mike's side throughout the service and afterwards, almost acting as hostess, much to Paul's chagrin. A married woman and a newly widowed man shouldn't seem so close. Others didn't seem to care, knowing that Marlene had been Christina's best friend. Mike acted uneasy, constantly glancing toward the door as if expecting someone to enter that he didn't want to see. Paul wondered if it was the police that he was worried about, or that his mistress would show up here and embarrass him. When the service was over, Marlene was sliding into her hired limo, noticed Mike looking around, and asked what was wrong.

"I'm looking for a phone both, I need to call a cab, I guess I should buy a car soon," he answered wearily.

"I'll give you a lift, where are you staying?" She reached for the door of the limo as she spoke.

"The Hilton," he answered, and her hand tightened. He was staying in the same hotel! Did she dare...? In light of the circumstances, she thought better of it.

"Right on our way, hop in." Paul saw them get into the limo together, and wondered if Marlene was actually the mistress in question. No, Christina would have told him. He shook his head and once again greeted and thanked people for coming. But he was glad when it was over so that he could go home to grieve in peace.

Chapter 23

Paul picked up the phone and dialed the police station. He asked for the detective that was investigating his daughter's death. He waited impatiently on hold, watching the minutes tick by.

"Detective Harrison here." Finally! Paul thought. He probably had to finish his donut, he noted sarcastically.

"This is Paul Solderburg, Christina Kingsbury's father. Did anyone tell you that my daughter had hired a private investigator to follow her husband?"

"Not that I'm aware of, Mr. Solderburg."

"Well, the pictures that he took are the reason that she threw the bum out. I thought you might want to talk to him. His name is Peter Wallace."

"Peter Wallace? Wasn't he fired for bribery or something like that?"

"Yes, I thought you might remember that name. Also, I have a more complete list of the jewelry that should have been in the safe, in case anyone tries to pawn it."

"Will you be home later? We can stop by and pick it up from you."

"Yes, I'll be home for the rest of the afternoon."

"Okay, we'll see you then."

"Thanks." Peter hung up the phone, his forehead creased with lines of strain.

"I'm going to be in the study," he mentioned to his housekeeper. "If someone comes from the police department, bring them in immediately." He made his way to his study and shut the door. He just needed a little time to himself, trying to get a grip on his emotions. How could someone do this to his little girl? Paul felt so empty inside, first his wife, now his daughter. The grief was almost too much to bear. He caught a glimpse of himself in the mirror; was it his imagination, or did he look older today than he did yesterday?

Meanwhile, Harrison told his partner, Detective Williams, what Solderburg had said on the phone. They agreed that they needed to get to Wallace as quickly as possible, and headed for his office. After showing their ID's to his secretary, they pushed open the door to his office. He looked up, curious.

"Can I help you, gentlemen?" His tone indicated that he was busy and did not appreciate them barging in as they had done.

"We need to ask you some questions, Wallace," said Williams as they flashed him their badges. They each grabbed a chair and sat across the desk from him.

"You were hired by a Mrs. Christina Kingsbury to follow her husband and get the dope on his affair, right?" the detective began.

"I don't think my client would appreciate me discussing her case, detective," Peter said with a sneer.

"I think your client is beyond caring about her case," Harrison sneered back. "She was robbed and killed late Friday night." Peter looked like someone had just punched him in the stomach.

"I had no idea, I was on a hunting trip and just got back last night" He sat and stared at the detectives as though willing them to tell him they believed him.

"Yes, she hired me to follow her husband. She suspected him, rightly, as it turned out, of having an affair. I took several pictures of him with a young woman in various locations, including a motel. When I gave her the pictures, she didn't have the money with her and was going to get cash the next day to pay me. I left the pictures, agreeing to come back the next day for the money. That night, Mr. Kingsbury showed up here and demanded the negatives. He talked me into selling them to him and then he burned them right here." He indicated the wastebasket, which still contained the ashes. "I went back to Mrs. Kingsbury for my fee, but she had allowed her husband to take her copies, and refused to pay me unless I made her another set. I intended to give her my file copies on Monday. I still haven't been paid for the job."

"Well, knowing you, you probably charged plenty for the negatives," Williams said crossly. "If I were you, I'd be happy with that. I doubt whoever inherits her estate is going to be too concerned with cleaning up this particular debt. Besides, it was a pretty dirty trick, selling the negatives to her husband." The detective twisted his face into a disgusted grimace.

"Getting canned from the force didn't get you to clean up your act at all?" the detective said, snidely.

"There's nothing illegal about selling pictures or negatives." Peter didn't like being reminded that he had been fired. "It's what I do for a living."

"We aren't talking legal, we're talking ethical," said Harrison, "When was the last time you saw Mrs. Kingsbury?"

"Just before noon on Friday. That's when I went to get my money, and she refused to pay me. Somehow, she found out about my selling the negatives to her husband. She went so far as to slam the door in my face." Only a slight exaggeration, he thought. No need to mention the veiled threat that he would get his money somehow. The last thing he needed right now was to be a suspect in a murder case. He would have to close his doors for good if that happened.

"Who else, besides Mr. Kingsbury, knew she'd hired you?" Williams still wasn't satisfied.

"I don't know. She asked me to be very discreet, I imagine she was, too. The household staff had to know I was at the house twice, whether she confided in them, I couldn't say. Maybe her father, those two are close."

"Yeah, well, don't let any of your cases take you out of town for awhile," the detectives rose, deliberately scraping their chairs across the floor as they did so. "You and your pictures may get called into court." They left without another word, almost slamming the door behind them. Peter rested his head on his folded arms. How and why had he ever gotten mixed up with the Kingsbury family?

Harrison and Williams decided they'd better find out exactly who had known about Wallace. They went to the Mallock home and rang the bell; Steven himself answered the door, he had given the nurse some time off.

"Mr. Mallock, just the person we need to see," one of the detectives pushed against the door, forcing Steven to step back. They entered the house, gesturing towards the back.

"Can we talk to you, perhaps in the kitchen?"

"Certainly, Detective, always glad to help." Steven led the way to the kitchen, glancing into his mother's bedroom as they passed to make sure the doorbell hadn't woken her.

"Now, what can I do for you?" he motioned for them to be seated, and took a chair himself.

"We've heard a few things that we would like you to confirm if possible," Harrison said, while Williams fished out the ever-present notebook.

"Such as?" Steven didn't sound particularly curious.

"Have you ever heard of a Mr. Peter Wallace?"

"Yes, of course," Steven said readily. "Mr. Wallace was at the house twice, no, three times. But the third time he was not invited in."

"Why was Mr. Wallace there?"

"I was not informed of Mr. Wallace's business at the house." Steven said in his most stuffy 'butler' voice.

"Yeah, right, can the Jeeves act, we ain't buyin' it," Harrison said sarcastically.

"Well, I did overhear something about following Mr. Kingsbury, and photographs, so I assumed he was a private investigator." Steven was not sure how much to tell them.

"The second time he came, I didn't hear anything."

"And the third time? The time he wasn't allowed in?"

"That time I was in the kitchen eating my lunch and didn't hear anything except the door slamming."

"Ok, now let's talk about Mr. Kingsbury. You were here when she threw him out? I though you left at nine-thirty every night?"

"It was early in the evening, he'd only been home about a half hour. Mrs. Kingsbury told me to take him anywhere he wanted to go, but not to bring him back."

"So you never saw the guy again?"

"Well, yeah, I saw him on Friday. He came around in a rental car, asking to see Mrs. Kingsbury. I told him he wasn't allowed on the premises, much less in the house. Told him I'd call the cops if he didn't beat it." Steven had become more sure of himself now.

"When was this? Late Friday?" Williams was writing in his notebook, while checking back to see what Kingsbury had said about his movements that night.

"No, around eight-thirty. I had washed the car, and was finishing up the polishing. I always wait until the sun is almost down, so it doesn't streak. After he left, and I went inside, it was nearly eight-forty-five."

"One more question, did the housekeeper, Nancy, also know who Mr. Wallace was?" Steven nodded.

"I told her myself."

"Thank you very much, Mallock, you've been very helpful." The detective sounded less than sincere. "I guess we know where to find you if we need you." The officers let themselves out.

Steven sat still for a moment, a thoughtful look on his face. Then he heard his mother calling him, and for the rest of the day he had no time to think. Harrison and Williams did, however, and the more they thought, the more they decided they should have another chat with Mr. Kingsbury. Mike groaned and opened one eye to look at the clock on the nightstand, then groaned again, someone was knocking on the door of his room and they weren't about to stop. He crawled out of bed and stumbled to the door.

"Who is it?" he asked angrily, "and what's so important?"

"Mr. Kingsbury, it's the police. Open the door, please." Sighing, Mike opened the door. The two detectives stepped into the room, followed by two uniformed officers, who immediately stepped up to Mike and took him by the arms.

"Mr. Kingsbury, you are under arrest for the murder of your wife", the detectives then proceeded to read him his Miranda rights. "Do you understand your rights as I have stated them?" Mike started to sputter.

"Yes, I understand." He asked for his clothes and his wallet. They allowed him to get dressed, then handcuffed him and led him to a waiting patrol car. Driving to the station, they tried to ask him more questions, but he wisely refused to open his mouth.

Arriving at the station, he was booked and fingerprinted, and was then told that he could call his lawyer. Sam Barber arrived looking a little tired, having been woken up from a sound sleep.

"What evidence do you have to arrest my client?" Sam turned to Williams to ask, once they were seated around the table.

"Well, for one thing, he neglected to mention that he tried to enter the house the day his wife was killed, and that he purchased the negatives to the pictures the detective took of him and his mistress. Among other things."

"What?" Sam was incredulous. He turned to Mike.

"What else haven't you told me?" he asked.

"Well, he probably didn't mention the scene he created in the liquor store when he found out that his wife had closed their account. Said she'd be sorry for it. Scared the clerk out of her wits, if I have it right."

"I didn't kill her!" Mike pounded on the table. "I went to see her to apologize. I was there before I went to the liquor store and from there I went straight back to the hotel."

"Look," said Harrison. "Paul Solderburg is really pushing the D.A. on this and he's all over us. If you've got something that absolutely proves you weren't here at the wrong time, we'd really like to hear about it." Mike dropped his head into his hands. Sam Barber closed his briefcase and inquired about bail.

"No bail," the detective stated, "Solderburg knows the judge, and convinced him the guy would bolt." Nodding in resignation, Sam left the station and Mike Kingsbury was led to his cell. Mike sat on the cot in disbelief. How would he get out of this? They already didn't believe him. Why had he lied about that day? Groaning, he lay down on the cot to think, and slowly drifted off to sleep.

Chapter 24

New York Criminal Court
Wednesday, July 22, 1992
10:00 AM

"All rise." Marlene rose with the rest of those present when the judge entered the courtroom. Mike was being arraigned for Christina's murder; she could hardly believe it. She sat in stunned silence as the prosecution outlined its case: the fight over Mike's affair, the photographs and burned negatives, the fact that Mike lied about his actions the night of the murder, and the scene in the liquor store. They brought up Christina's money, Mike's large withdrawal, and the fact that he had access to the bedroom safe, they even mentioned the fact that Mike had chosen the most expensive hotel in town to live in. The prosecution called a Forensics expert who stated that Christina had been killed around midnight. He revealed that the evidence found clenched in her right hand was wool and polyester fibers, commonly found in hats and ski masks. The only fingerprints found in the bedroom belonged to the couple and their housekeeper, with the exception of Paul Solderburg's on the doorknob. An expert was called who demonstrated how the injury proved that she had been near the door when she had been pushed and was falling when she hit the mantle.

"So, the last thing Christina saw as she died was the face of her killer?" the Prosecutor asked the expert in a final, dramatic moment.

"Yes, that would be true," replied the witness.

"I have no further questions, Your Honor." The Prosecutor returned to his chair.

It did not take the court long to decide that the state had enough evidence for a trial. Mike was denied bail again, and the trial date was set for October Sixth. Marlene held back tears as she watched them lead Mike away. She had never felt so helpless. As she turned to go, she caught Paul's eye; he did not look happy to see her there. Then she saw him look past her and really frown. She followed his line of sight, and saw a man she didn't recognize talking to one of the court personnel. Looking around, she spotted Steven and Nancy, and a very lovely young woman standing apart from everyone else. Holding her breath, she wondered if this was Mike's mistress. The woman felt her staring and looked up. When she met Marlene's eyes, she turned red and hurried from the room, confirming Marlene's suspicions. Marlene felt more depressed than ever, and went back to her hotel to pack for home.

Paul made his way over to the man he had been frowning at.

"Wallace, what are you doing here?" Paul demanded.

"I have a vested interest in this case, Mr. Solderburg," Peter stated calmly. "Your daughter never paid me for the work I did, but that doesn't lessen my obligation to come forward with evidence that may put away her killer." He turned to go, but Solderburg stopped him.

"So, she owed you money, huh? How do we know YOU didn't go after it that night? Ex-police, private investigator, you wouldn't have any trouble with alarms, would you?" he accused.

"Mr. Solderburg," Detective Harrison said, pulling Paul's hand off of Peter's arm. "Let us do the investigating, will you? Believe me, if we had reason to believe Wallace was involved, he'd be right in that cell next to Kingsbury." Paul looked from Harrison to Williams, who suddenly appeared next to Harrison.

"Well, as long as you are still on the case..." Paul turned on his heel and left the courtroom.

"We should keep an eye on everyone involved. Maybe we

were too hasty in arresting Kingsbury," Harrison said to Williams.

"The case ain't closed until it's closed, partner." The detectives then also left the courtroom, holding the door open for Steven and Nancy, who were the last ones out. Sam Barber was standing in the hallway.

"Good luck, Counselor," Harrison and Williams said as they passed. He did not even look up.

New York Criminal Court
November 6th 1992

"All rise." David Larson of the state's District Attorney's office rose to his feet. He was not particularly tall, but he chose his clothes well, and was an imposing figure. Beside him was Anita Templeton, fairly new to the office, but capable nonetheless and a good few inches shorter, which is why he had requested her on this case. In his experience, jury members were sometimes swayed by the impression the lawyer made rather than by hard evidence. Looking across at the defense table, he noticed Sam Barber looking a little grim, and his partner a little nervous. Mike Kingsbury just looked scared. The judge read the report of the case, and asked the prosecution to make his opening remarks. As David spoke, he watched the faces of the jurors; it was as if they were trying to tell whether or not Mike was a murderer just by the clothes he wore. He played up the dramatic angle of the case, the argument, the investigation, even the fact that Christina was one of the richest women in the city, and Mike was "just" an architect. Marlene, sitting behind Paul, was appalled.

"How could he make Mike sound so guilty when the trial has barely started?" she thought to herself. During Sam Barber's opening remarks, however, Marlene began to relax. Sam sounded so logical, she was sure he would be able to prove that Mike was not guilty. If only she could convince Paul, but he was so determined to see Mike punished for his daughter's death, she doubted he would listen to anyone. With both attorneys wanting to sway the jurors to their side, the opening remarks took all morning. Finally, the judge called the noon recess.

Over lunch, Marlene nearly bit through her tongue trying not to contradict Paul at the next table. He complained about everything, he didn't know the judge, he didn't like a woman on the prosecution team, and on and on. The only thing he seemed to approve of was the appointment of David Larson to the case. Calling him "the best damn lawyer in the state".

"He'll see that bum fry, you mark my words," he added. It was a relief to return to the courtroom. The prosecution called as their first witness, Nancy Clapper, the housekeeper.

"Did you see Mike Kingsbury after the night he was asked to leave?" she was asked, after describing the finding of the body.

"No, sir, not personally," she hesitated, "I was told that he had been there, but I didn't see him."

"Did you hear anything that night, after you retired to your room?"

"No, sir, my room is in the basement. Mrs. Kingsbury has, well, had, an intercom in her room if she needed me at night."

"One more question, Mrs. Clapper," Larson said gently. "Did Mr. Kingsbury know the alarm codes and the safe combination?"

"Yes, sir, he did. Mrs. Kingsbury had mentioned having them changed, but hadn't done it yet." "Thank you, Nancy. Your witness, Counselor." Sam Barber rose to his feet.

"No questions, Your Honor," he stated without leaving the defense table, and sat back down. The judge told Nancy she could step down, and Larson called Steven Mallock to the stand.

"You were the one who drove Mr. Kingsbury away from the house the day before these events, were you not?" he was asked, after reciting his actions the night and morning in question.

"Yes, sir. I was told to take him anywhere he wanted to go, but not to bring him back." Steven supplied.

"Isn't it true that you were specifically requested not to let him enter the house ever again?"

"Yes, sir. As soon as I arrived back to the house, Mrs. Kingsbury told me that."

"And did you ever have an opportunity to exercise those instructions?" the Prosecutor probed.

"Yes, sir, the same night Mrs. Kingsbury died about eight-thirty. Mr. Kingsbury drove up in a rented car, and asked if Mrs. Kingsbury was at home. I told him I couldn't let him in, and that I would call the police if he didn't leave. He left at that point."

"Where did he ask you to take him the night he left the house – the first time?"

"Well, at first, he just said drive toward the city, but after I mentioned Mr. Wallace, he asked to be taken to the Hilton."

"The Hilton?" David Larson feigned surprise. Almost as if he were speaking to himself, he added "Pretty fancy for a guy who's been thrown out with nothing."

"Objection, counsel is leading the witness!" Sam Barber was indignant.

"That wasn't a question, Counselor," Larson smirked

"Nonetheless," the judge stated, "objection sustained. Counsel will refrain from personal comments during questioning."

"I apologize, Your Honor," David said smoothly.

"Now, Mr. Mallock, how was it that you happened to mention Mr. Wallace to Mr. Kingsbury?"

"Mr. Kingsbury asked me if Mrs. Kingsbury had any visitors that day."

"And you felt obliged to tell him, even though Mrs. Kingsbury's father pays your salary?" Sam Barber started to rise.

"Never mind, I withdraw the question. Your witness, Counselor." Barber seemed a little unsure how to proceed.

"You said you told Mr. Kingsbury that you would call the police if he didn't leave. Did he, in fact, make any attempt to enter the house?"

"Well, no, sir, not exactly. I moved in front of him when he got out of his car, and he stopped. When I told him he wasn't allowed in, and about the police, he just climbed back in his car and drove off."

"No arguing, no threats?"

"No, sir"

"What time did you say this was?"

"About eight-thirty. When I finished cleaning the car and retired for the evening, it was quarter to nine."

"Thank you, Mr. Mallock." The judge excused him; he stepped down and left the courtroom. David Larson rose to his feet.

"Your Honor, we anticipate a quite lengthy examination for our next witness, and would prefer to have it uninterrupted. Therefore, we request court be adjourned until tomorrow."

"Since it's after three, I will grant that request. Court is adjourned until ten tomorrow morning."

"At least," thought Marlene grimly as she rose for the judge's entrance into court the next morning, "we are getting our exercise with all of this standing and sitting." She and Paul Solderburg were once again present in the courtroom. She was slightly amazed that neither the prosecution nor the defense had called either of them as a witness, but since that would allow her to see the entire trial, she was not about to volunteer. She was determined not to miss a minute. Paul had made the same comment, but she knew he was hoping that Mike would be convicted, while she was hoping for the opposite verdict. She focused on the witness stand as a man was being sworn in, and heard him state his name as Peter Wallace. It was the same man that Paul had been so upset to see the day of the arraignment, but who was he? The man sat down, and David Larson approached the stand.

"Mr. Wallace, you are a licensed Private Investigator in the state of New York, are you not?"

"That is correct." Mr. Wallace looked quite at home, as if he was no stranger to a courtroom.

"You were acquainted with both the defendant and the victim, is that correct also?"

"Well, yes, in a manner of speaking."

"Please explain to the court your relationship to the deceased." David Larson looked at the jury as if to ask them to pay close attention to this witness.

"In April of this year, I received a call at my office from a Christina Kingsbury, who stated that she required some discreet investigation work. I went out to see her at her home and agreed to do the job. I saw her again when I took her the results of my investigation, and again when I went back to collect my fee."

"Thank you, Mr. Wallace. Now, please explain what that discreet investigation consisted of, exactly." Peter shifted in his chair. It was obvious he did not want to talk about this part.

"Well, she suspected that her husband was having an affair. I was instructed to follow him and provide proof one way or the other."

"And the results of this investigation?"

"I took several pictures of Mr. Kingsbury with a young blond woman, a very striking blond, in fact.

"I believe you have my file copies..." David held a hand up to stop him from going further, and turned to the prosecutor's table, where Anita Templeton was holding out a stack of pictures.

"Your Honor, the people wish to enter into evidence these photographs. They have a date/time stamp on them, and the name 'Wallace Investigations' printed on the back." The judge took the photos, looked through them briefly, and then handed them to the bailiff to be marked.

"Are these the photographs you took for Mrs. Kingsbury?" Larson asked after the bailiff returned the photos to him. Peter took them and glanced through them.

"Yes, these are the ones. I always keep a copy for my files."

"Was there any one picture that Mrs. Kingsbury seemed particularly interested in or upset by?"

"Objection!" Sam was rising to his feet, but the judge stopped him.

"Objection overruled. As a trained investigator, Mr. Wallace is an expert at observing people and their reactions. I will allow the question."

"You will answer the question, sir," the judge instructed Peter.

"Well," Peter frowned, trying to remember. He was apparently not expecting this to come up. "There was one – if I could just have a moment – yes! Here it is." He handed a picture to David Larson."She went back to this one after she had seen them all. She looked at it very closely, and then asked if I knew who the woman was."

"We'll get back to that in a minute, Mr. Wallace. Meanwhile, I want to show this picture to the jury, if it please the court." The judge looked at Sam Barber as if expecting an objection, then nodded at Larson to continue. Larson handed the photo to the jury foreman, who passed it down the line. Marlene found herself wishing she could see it. Why hadn't Christina confided her fears about Mike? As she sat, trying to absorb this latest shock, David Larson began to speak again.

"Now, Mr. Wallace, you stated that Mrs. Kingsbury did not ask you who the woman was until after she had seen this picture. Did you indeed know who the woman was?"

"Not at that time. I have since discovered her identity."

"As part of your investigation?"

"No, sir, quite by accident. I saw her picture in the paper."

"I see." David Larson set the pictures down on the prosecutor's table. Marlene could now see the photograph on top. It was a close-up of Mike kissing a woman's neck. The same woman she had seen in the courtroom yesterday; she had been right about her identity! What was more, the woman was wearing earrings just like the ones Christina had misplaced. Was it possible that Mike had...no, she refused to believe that. It was a coincidence, it had to be. She re-focused on what Mr. Wallace was saying. He had been asked to explain his relationship to Mike.

"The day I took Mrs. Kingsbury the pictures, I went back to my office to work on some paperwork. At about eight-thirty, the after hours line rang. It was Mr. Kingsbury, although I didn't know it at the time. I'd never gotten close enough to hear his voice during my investigation. Anyway, he said he had urgent business that couldn't wait. The guy sounded desperate, so I agreed to see him. When he showed up, and I saw who it was, I told him I couldn't help him."

"But you did help him, did you not, Mr. Wallace?"

"Well, yes," he admitted. He was decidedly uncomfortable now. "He wanted the negatives from the pictures I had taken for his wife. Since I hadn't been paid for them, I guess I felt justified in selling the negatives."

"Where are those negatives now?"

"Kingsbury burned them. Right there in front of me. In my wastebasket."

"Did Mr. Kingsbury state a reason that he wanted those negatives destroyed?"

"He said that they would be evidence if his wife decided to actually divorce him, and he wanted them destroyed. I don't know what he did with the pictures he had."

"Thank you, Mr. Wallace," David was almost smug.

"Your witness, Counselor." Sam Barber seemed a bit shell-shocked. He got to his feet, then hesitated and looked through some notes. Finally, he approached the witness stand.

"Mr. Wallace, what day was it that you were hired by Mrs. Kingsbury?"

"Friday, May 9th," he said promptly. Sam raised one eyebrow.

"You remember that precisely?" Sam asked surprised.

"I assumed I would be asked, I looked up the file this morning."

"I see. And when did you take her the photographs?"

"On May 13th."

"And you stated that you had to go back a third time?"

"Yes. Mrs. Kingsbury didn't want to write a check, and she had forgotten to get cash. She asked me to come back the next day for my money."

"So, you returned the day that she was killed? At what time?"

"In the morning. I know it was before noon, because I arrived at my office just as my secretary was leaving for lunch."

"And Mrs. Kingsbury had the money ready for you?"

"Well..." he was really starting to squirm now. "No, she refused to pay me."

"But you had done what she hired you to do, why would she refuse?"

"She had figured out that her husband had bought the negatives. He had also gotten hold of her copy of the pictures, so she had nothing. She refused to pay me until I got her another set."

"Did that make you angry?"

"Objection, Your Honor. I fail to see where this has relevance to the case." David protested. The judge looked thoughtfully at Sam.

"Counselor, does this have relevance?"

"The state has tried to present this as a black and white case, Your Honor, with all the good being on the side of the victim. I am merely trying to expose some shades of gray. Perhaps Mrs. Kingsbury was not the saint she has been portrayed to be. Perhaps, also, there is more than one person with a motive of money."

"I'll allow it, but be careful, Counselor. The victim is not on trial here, nor is the witness."

"Yes, Your Honor. Now, Mr. Wallace, did the fact that Mrs. Kingsbury refused to pay you for work you had already done make you angry at her?"

"Well, yes. But as it was pointed out later, the amount I received for the negatives more than made up for it."

"How much later?"

"I beg your pardon?" Peter asked confused.

"Was this pointed out to you before or after Mrs. Kingsbury was killed?"

"Your Honor!" Now it was David Larson's turn to leap to his feet.

"I withdraw the question, Your Honor. I have no further questions of this witness."

"Re-direct, Counselor?" the judge asked the prosecution.

"Thank you, Your Honor, just one question." He stood and walked toward Wallace.

"When was the last time you saw Mrs. Kingsbury, Mr. Wallace?"

"Friday morning, just before she slammed her front door on me," Peter said dryly. "And she was very much alive."

"Thank you," Larson sat down. Peter Wallace was excused from the stand.

The next witness called was also a stranger to Marlene. When he had been sworn in and stated his name, David Larson asked him his occupation.

"I operate a state liquor store," the man stated. Mike seemed to sink further down in his chair. Marlene wondered what he was so nervous about with this witness.

"Have you ever seen the defendant?" Larson asked the man.

"Yes, Sir, he came into my store a while back."

"How long ago, do you recall?"

"Not exactly. Some time in April this year." David took a piece of paper from the prosecution table.

"Your Honor, the people wish to enter into evidence this printout from a credit card machine. It clearly shows that Mr. Kingsbury was in fact in the liquor store at eight-fifty-three p.m. on the night in question." He handed the paper to the judge, who went through the same procedure as with the photos earlier. David turned back to the witness.

"Now having established when the defendant was in your store, would you please tell the court what happened that night?"

"Sure," the man seemed to relish the spotlight. "He came in, like I said, grabbed a bottle of very expensive whiskey. I was in the back, but I came out when the racket started."

"Racket?' inquired Larson.

"Yeah. This guy," the man pointed at Mike, "was carrying on something awful. Yelling about how some...you'll pardon the expression, Your Honor, some bitch had closed their bank account.

Seems he tried to pay for his bottle with his bank debit card and it didn't go through. He said she would be sorry she had done it." Then he paid cash for the bottle and left.

"Was anyone else in the store at the time?"

"No other customers. We were just about to close. Everyone in the neighborhood knows when we close; they get there earlier. Just me and my cashier were there."

"Your Honor," David turned to the judge. "We would be willing to put the cashier on the stand if necessary, but she is eight months pregnant, and we'd rather avoid the stress it would cause her. We do have her signed affidavit here." He produced some papers from his briefcase and handed them to the judge, who perused them.

"Let the record show that the affidavit from the cashier confirms the store manger's testimony," announced the judge. "Unless there is some reason the defense needs to hear it?" He looked over at Sam Barber, who rose and stated that he did not need the cashier in court.

"Just one more question, then," David Larson turned back to the witness. "When Mr. Kingsbury left your store, did he get into the driver's seat, or the passenger seat of the car he arrived in with his whisky bottle?" The judge looked over at Barber again, clearly expecting him to object to this question, but he was quiet. The witness stated that Mike had gotten into the driver's seat. Larson announced that he had no further questions. Barber had no questions of this witness. The next two witnesses called by the prosecution were Harrison and Williams, the two detectives who were investigating the crime. In the course of questioning, it was revealed that Mike had told the police he had taken a taxi everywhere that night, when in fact, he had rented a car. David Larson managed to make much of the fact that he had omitted to tell the police that he had stopped by the house, and also that he had never revealed the name of the 'friend' he had drinks with that night. Finally, they were both excused, and Larson called one last witness. He identified himself as Christina's personal lawyer.

Larson stepped up to the stand and paused.

"Is it not true that the Kingsburys signed a pre-nuptial agreement?" the prosecution asked once the courtroom was silent. A collective gasp rippled through everyone seated in the courtroom. The judge banged his gavel and called for order.

"Answer the question please," the judge instructed the witness.

"Yes, my client's father recommended it. They signed it three days before they were married. I gave you a copy of it yesterday." Larson reached for the papers Anita was holding out.

"Your Honor, the people wish to enter into evidence this agreement between the defendant and his late wife, the victim in this case." When the process was complete, he turned back to the witness.

"Now then, can you give us a synopsis of this agreement?"

"Well, basically, it lists all of Christina's assets before her marriage, and states that in the case of a divorce, Mr. Kingsbury would be entitled to none of these assets, nor any portion of any gifts received by Mrs. Kingsbury from any party, including himself."

"So, in layman's terms, all the jewelry in the safe, and probably a good portion of the money, also, he wouldn't be able to touch if they were divorced?"

"That is almost correct, sir. Although the bank account that she closed was in both of their names, all the money in it had been Christina's. Mr. Kingsbury's money went into his business accounts. He would not have received any of it."

"That's all fine and good, but we also have another document to discuss, here." He turned and took it from Anita. "The Last Will and Testament of Christina Solderburg Kingsbury," he read. "We would like to also enter this into evidence, Your Honor." Once that had been done, he again approached the witness.

"Briefly outline this document, if you will, sir."

"It's just the opposite," stated the lawyer. "Mrs. Kingsbury left everything to her husband in the event of her death. Everything." The emphasis on the last word echoed through the minds of the jurors.

"So, she divorces him, he gets nothing, but she dies, he gets everything?" David asked after a long pause, letting the implication sink in.. The witness nodded.

"I'm sorry, sir, you'll have to speak up, the court clerk can't hear a nod."

"Yes," the lawyer stated. "That is an accurate assessment of the situation."

"Thank you. Your witness, Counselor." Sam Barber just sat there. How could he have forgotten about the pre-nuptial? This was going to sound the death knell on Mike!

"Counselor?" The judge was asking him to cross-examine. He managed to make it to his feet.

"No questions, Your Honor." He sank back in to his seat, only to rise again when the judge adjourned for the day. He turned to Mike, who was white as a sheet.

"You should have reminded me about this," Sam whispered.

"I forgot, too," Mike whispered back. Sam wasn't sure if he believed that or if he still believed his friend was innocent. With a heavy heart, he watched them lead Mike away.

Chapter 25

"Your Honor, the state would like to call as its next witness Miss Judy Brown." There was a rustling in the courtroom. This was a name that had not yet been mentioned, who was she? The witness door opened and in walked a beautiful young woman. Marlene held back a gasp. Mike's mistress! She frowned as she watched Miss Brown walk across the courtroom to the witness stand. David Larson didn't miss a trick; he had apparently asked her to wear what she had been wearing in the picture that had already been shown to the jury. Same blouse, hairstyle, even those earrings. Again Marlene wondered if Mike was capable of giving someone else Christina's earrings, then replacing them. She tried to clear her mind so that she could concentrate on Miss Brown's testimony.

"State your occupation, please."

"I am the Architectural Coordinator for the City of New York, Manhattan Borough."

"As such, you were responsible for the construction permits involved in the municipal pool project that has spanned the last year, were you not?"

"That is correct," Judy replied.

"Explain your relationship to the defendant."

"Mr. Kingsbury is one of the owners of the firm that had the contract for the municipal pool."

"I'm aware of the that, but that does not fully answer the question. Please do so, Miss Brown."

"Objection. Counsel is badgering his own witness." Sam announced, not even bothering to stand up. David Larson turned to the judge.

"Your Honor, once Miss Brown fully answers the question, it will become apparent that she could be considered a hostile witness. I request being allowed to continue in this vein." The judge appeared to consider the request. He looked at Miss Brown, then recognition dawned.

"Objection overruled. Witness will answer the question." Larson turned back to the stand, and leaned closer to Judy.

"Now, Miss Brown, please fully explain your relationship to the defendant." Judy seemed to shrink a little in her seat.

"I am...was...his girlfriend," she admitted slowly.

"Was?" David seemed taken aback. "And when exactly did this relationship end?"

"Two days before he was arrested."

"I see. Miss Brown, those are lovely earrings you are wearing, where did you get them?"

Barber started to speak, then shook his head. Judy turned pale and hesitated before answering.

"I...they were a gift from a friend," she said defiantly.

"A friend named Mike Kingsbury, true?" Larson was obviously becoming impatient.

"Did he or did he not give them to you the day of the groundbreaking for the pool?" Both Judy and Mike seemed surprised at this question.

"I...I don't remember when..." Judy stammered.

Larson made a face.

"Miss Brown, I can call a witness from your office that will testify that you were not wearing those earrings before the ceremony, but you were wearing them when you came back from lunch. Are you going to make that necessary?"

"No." Judy seemed crestfallen. "Mike gave me the earrings that day."

"Were you aware that these earrings are identical in size and shape to the earrings he gave to his wife for her birthday last year?"

"No, I didn't know that." Judy looked over at Mike questioningly.

"Earrings that we have been told disappeared briefly around Halloween last year from Christina's bedroom, and were 'found' in a box from a different jeweler," he added accusingly.

"Objection!" Barber could stand it no longer. "This is all speculation on the part of the State."

"On the contrary, Your Honor," Larson was already pulling papers out of his briefcase. "We decided to investigate what would have upset Mrs. Kingsbury so much about that particular picture, so we took it to show her housekeeper. When she saw the date, she told us about the earrings; we have a signed affidavit. We will recall her to the stand if Counselor insists." The judge took and read the affidavit, then handed it to the bailiff.

"Objection overruled." Larson turned back to Judy.

"Miss Brown, you were aware of the defendant's marital state when you began your relationship with him, were you not?" David asked, appearing to barely have his anger under control.

"Well, yes, but..." Judy was turning red, from anger or embarrassment – it was hard to tell. "Well, it started out so innocently. We had architecture in common, and he could talk to me." She looked down at her hands clenched on her lap.

"Before I knew it, I started to fall in love. I knew he was in love with me. He told me he was going to leave her, that he had to figure out a way to do it and still get some money out of the deal, that all the money was hers. He said that he had been mesmerized by her wealth, but that he was truly in love for the first time – with me."

"If that is the case, why did you break off the relationship? After all, his wife is gone, he would apparently inherit..."

"I didn't!" Judy sat up straight and fixed Larson with a glare. "Mike said it would be best if we broke it off for a while until things cooled down. He said that if everyone knew about us, well, he said that they would..."

"Suspect him of killing his wife?" David suggested ironically.

Judy nodded, unable to speak. Her eyes filled with tears, and she began to grope in her skirt pocket. David snorted as if to say 'well, we did anyway', but didn't voice the thought out loud. He turned to Barber.

"Your witness. Counselor." He managed to make it sound as if he was saying, 'good luck with this one'. Sam Barber rose to his feet.

"Miss Brown, do you feel that you can go on with this?" Judy dried her eyes with a tissue and nodded, raising her head to look at him. She did not look at Mike again.

"Miss Brown, you had no idea that those were his wife's earrings, did you?" Sam asked her gently.

"No, sir, Mike said they were thanks for all my hard work getting the permits in time. Honestly, when he gave them to me, I wasn't even sure they were real." Judy said, pleading, hoping the judge believed her.

"Whose idea was it to take the relationship from business to personal, yours or Mr. Kingsbury's?" Judy's mouth fell open. She had never expected this question. Now they were going to try to make her out to be a home wrecker. Would they suspect her of murder next? She blinked and realized Barber was speaking again.

"Miss Brown, answer the question please."

"Well, I'm not sure..." she began. Sam wheeled around and took a piece of green paper from his assistant. He held it up and stated that he wanted it entered into evidence; the bailiff processed the paper and returned it to the defense.

"Do you recognize this, Miss Brown?" Judy burst into tears. "It's a note I wrote. Alright, I'll admit that I suggested it first. But Mike didn't exactly fight the idea. It was at that lunch that he gave me the earrings." While she had been testifying, Mike had been looking more and more dejected. This was not going well. Now he knew what it was like to "fight City Hall". Paul Solderburg's money had insured that the State left no stone unturned in its investigation. Even the things he thought would be in his favor were being turned around to condemn him. He brought his mind back to the present in time to hear David Larson state that he had no re-direct for Miss Brown, and she was excused from the stand.

"In light of the fact that it is almost eleven-thirty, we will recess for lunch. Counsel, are you prepared to proceed this afternoon?" the judge asked Sam.

"Yes, Your Honor," Barber confirmed.

"Very well, then, court stands in recess."

At lunch, Marlene could hardly choke down her food. How in the world was Mike's lawyer going to present a defense in the face of all this? She, too, knew that Paul was responsible for the thoroughness of the case against Mike. Why was he so sure Mike was guilty? For that matter, why was she so sure Mike was innocent?

When court re-convened, the defense called as their first two witnesses men from Mike's architectural firm. The idea was to paint Mike as a hard-working man, despite his wife's money. They testified that he worked hard, sometimes late and on weekends; he never assigned anyone a job he himself would not be willing to do, and he was very generous with his employees. However, on cross-examination, David Larson got them to admit that Mike had been taking longer and longer lunches, spent a lot of time in afternoon 'meetings' that no one ever heard any results from, and was less attentive to things in the last six months before his arrest. In fact, one of them admitted that the rumors about Mike and Judy were pretty much accepted around the office as gospel truth. Larson produced credit card receipts proving that Mike frequented several hotels around town during the day. He also produced his company credit card records and expense statement, which contained expenditures that were obviously of a personal nature, but were written off as business using Judy's title instead of her name. The end result was that these "character witnesses" shredded what was left of Mike's character. Barber felt totally defeated.

"Your Honor, Defense calls as its next witness Mr. Robert

Hamish." Mike didn't recognize the name, but he did recognize the man who came in as the night clerk at the Hilton. He brightened up a little. This man had been delighted to have a Kingsbury in 'his' hotel, and had always treated Mike like visiting royalty. His testimony was bound to be positive.

"State your occupation, please." Sam instructed.

"I run the desk at the Hilton Hotel in the evenings, Sir," the man said. "I'm off duty Mondays and Tuesdays." Sam Barber suppressed a smile.

"Thank you. Now, do you recognize the defendant?"

"Oh, yes, sir, that's Mr. Kingsbury. We have been privileged to have him as a guest in the past. When I got the call from your office, I looked up the records. He stayed with us from the evening of May 14th until...well...his unfortunate acquaintance with our police force," he testified.

"And were you on duty every night he stayed at your hotel?"

"Yes, sir! We spoke every evening as he came in from work, sir. That's why Friday sticks out in my mind so clearly."

"Explain that, if you please."

"Well, he didn't come back to the hotel to change after work that night. In fact, he didn't return until after ten-thirty that evening."

"And did he say anything when he came in?" Sam questioned.

"Just asked for his messages. There were two. I couldn't talk at the time anyway, my manager had come in to check on some paperwork, and he was still at the front desk." He paused briefly and looked a little sheepish. "We're not encouraged to become too familiar with the guests."

"But you're sure of the time?"

Oh, yes, sir, I looked at the clock. I had been wondering what had happened to keep him so late, so it was an automatic gesture. I normally don't keep track of a guest, but Mr. Kingsbury had been very friendly."

"I understand. Thank you, I have no further questions." Sam Barber was really discouraged now. This testimony was supposed to have given Mike an alibi, but instead, it proved he had none for the time of death. Where in the world had he been between the liquor store and the hotel? David Larson had no questions for the witness, and he was excused. Before the judge could announce that it was time for closing remarks, David Larson stood up.

"If it please the court," he began, "one of our previous witnesses has come forth with new information that we think needs to be heard." The judge hesitated briefly.

"Very well, Counsel may recall this witness."

"Thank you, Your Honor. The State calls back to the stand Mrs. Nancy Clapper." Nancy entered the courtroom and approached the witness stand. She started to raise her hand, but the judge stated that she was still under oath. Nervously, she nodded and sat down. Larson approached her slowly.

"Mrs. Clapper," he said, "You called Detective Harrison this morning because you had remembered something about the case, is this correct?" David asked her gently.

"Yes, sir. It occurred to me as I was walking into the kitchen this morning."

"Suppose you repeat for the court what you remembered."

"Well, the night that Mrs. Kingsbury was... killed, I had gone downstairs, but I had forgotten my glass of water. You see, I have to take a pill every morning when I wake up, and I always take a glass of water with me to my room at night." Nancy paused to take a deep breath, and Larson nodded at her encouragingly.

"Well, as I stepped into the kitchen that night, I thought I heard Mrs. Kingsbury's voice, so I stopped to listen. I thought that she was just trying to figure out who was up and I was going to reply that it was just me. Before I could say anything, I heard her say 'Mike, is that you?' I thought she was maybe having a nightmare. I listened for a minute, but she didn't say anything else, so I got my water and went back to bed. If only I'd gone upstairs and checked..." She looked as though she would burst into tears, and Larson stepped up and handed her a tissue, saying,

"Now, Nancy, you couldn't have known." She sniffled and

134

nodded, and tried to smile at him.

"I have no further questions. Your witness, Counselor." Barber stood and approached Nancy.

"Mrs. Clapper, did you hear any other voices besides Mrs. Kingsbury's?"

"No, sir, just hers."

"No one answered her question with a positive or a negative?" Sam probed.

She looked up at him, puzzled.

"No one said, 'yes, it's me' or 'no, it's not'?" Sam rephrased the question, seeing her confusion.

"No, sir, I heard no answer at all."

"So you couldn't say for sure there was anyone there at all. In fact, your first instinct was that she was having a nightmare, is that correct?"

"Yes, sir, I didn't think anyone else was in the house."

"Thank you, Nancy. I have no further questions, Your Honor." Sam returned to his seat feeling more sure of himself now. The judge told Nancy to step down, and then announced that it was time for closing remarks.

Larson literally ripped Mike to shreds, calling him a philandering gold-digger with no respect for marriage vows; reminding the jury that he had not been honest with the police or his lawyer, playing up the temper angle. Barber's momentary sense of satisfaction was gone. His remarks consisted mainly of the phrase 'circumstantial evidence'. Sam tried to cast doubt on Peter Wallace's credentials, and pointedly reiterated the fact that Mike had left peacefully earlier in the evening. As he spoke, he watched the faces of the jurors, and his heart sank. They had already made up their minds. It didn't take long for the jury to reach a verdict of 'guilty'.

The judge announced sentencing for Tuesday, December 22nd, 1992. On that day at eleven a.m., Mike Kingsbury was sentenced to life in prison for the murder of his wife, Christina.

Chapter 26

Mike opened his eyes and started to talk, Jane and Anita listening eagerly,

"The first time I brought her a white rose, she cried for a long time." He was talking more to himself now than Jane, reminiscing. "Her father would bring her one with a pearl every birthday. She was going to pass those pearls down to her daughter, but we never had time to start a family. I suppose the killer got them?" This last remark was addressed to Anita, who nodded. "That's all I can think of for now. If I come up with anything else important, how do I contact you?" Jane told him to just get word to Anita; she would know how to reach her.

"Afraid to let a con have your phone number, huh, Doc?" Mike grinned at her. "Might not look good to your patients."

"I'm not from New York," she said patiently. "It would be difficult for you to reach me from here. I do appreciate your help. I may come back if I have any questions that only you can answer."

"Well, you know where to find me," he said, half joking. Anita motioned to the guard, and he escorted Mike back the way he had come.

The two women returned to Anita's car. As they drove away from the prison yard, Anita turned to Jane.

"I wish you hadn't told him quite so much. What if we can't prove he's not guilty? I don't even know if Larson will re-open the case on the say-so of a sixteen-year-old girl who hit her head."

"I'm not asking him to. I'm trying to get something solid enough to make him want to re-open the case. What if Kingsbury is innocent? Can your conscience allow you to just shrug it off? I didn't believe Claire at first either. I thought she was just trying to get attention. But now, I'm beginning to believe there's something going on that I can't explain. Whether it's reincarnation, or Christina reaching out from the grave to right a wrong, it can't be ignored." Anita sighed.

"Ok, what else do you need from me?"

"I need photographs. Everyone that was involved in the trial, Christina's father, even people that just showed up to watch. Maybe one of them is the killer." Anita frowned.

"I will have to get permission to remove them from the files."

"All I need is copies. I want to show them to Claire and see whom she recognizes." Anita agreed to check, and dropped Jane off at her hotel. Jane spent the afternoon organizing her thoughts and her notes from her visit with Mike Kingsbury. Anita was busier. As soon as she got back to her office, she called Larson's office and asked if she could see him right away. She didn't beat around the bush.

"David, I have to talk to you about the Kingsbury case."

"Kingsbury? That was...Anita, that was fifteen years ago!" he exclaimed.

"Sixteen, but I have reason to believe that there is a possibility that we convicted the wrong man," she argued.

"New evidence? Strong enough to re-open the case? It was almost open and shut, as I recall."

"I have an old college friend who lives out in Washington State. She has a sixteen-year-old patient who claims that she remembers being Christina Kingsbury, and that her husband didn't kill her." David was silent for a minute, and then he burst out laughing.

"Oh, Anita, I thought you were serious! Haven't you looked at the calendar? April Fools' Day was almost a month ago. Kingsbury is as guilty as the day is long."

"I'm not joking, David. I remember the case, too. It was my first court case, and I remember thinking at the time that there wasn't much of a defense. What if we all let Solderburg's pressuring get to us, and didn't spend enough time trying to find the truth once we had Kingsbury? You're the DA now, and Solderburg is dead. You are the one with the power in this office. Can you ignore the possibility that he might be innocent?" As she echoed Jane's words, she realized that she truly believed them. Now all she wanted was to know the truth, and Claire just might have it. But could she convince David Larson?

"Ok, tell me about this Girl and the CONNECTION," Larson said reluctantly.

"She was born the same night Christina was murdered. Jane believes that she may be Christina reincarnated. When we talked to Mike Kingsbury this morning..."

"You what?" Anita had his full attention now. "Don't tell me you told him you might be getting him out?" he groaned.

"It was the only way to get him to answer questions. He has no reason to trust me. But once Jane told him we might be able to prove his innocence, he cooperated."

"Be very careful with this, Anita. If the press gets hold of it before we really have a case, we could go down fast. We need something concrete," David warned her.

"Exactly why I came to you. We have photographs on file of everyone connected with the case, including all the witnesses, Solderburg, and both the Kingsburys. I want permission to loan them to Jane so she can show them to Claire to test her recollection." Larson did not hesitate.

"No way. You're not opening that file, and you are not removing anything." He was almost yelling now.

"What are you afraid of, David? We did our job, and the jury convicted him. How could a little digging hurt? If he's found innocent, you will look like a hero setting him free and admitting we made a mistake. If you refuse to investigate, and the press finds out..." she coerced.

"Alright!" Larson could tell when he'd been outmaneuvered. "But I want an exact accounting of every photo she takes, and she takes ONLY photos. No transcripts, no other evidence."

"Yes, sir!" Anita saluted smartly and left the room before David could change his mind.

Anita went down to the file room and located the case. Picking out one photo of each person involved, she signed them out and jubilantly headed for Jane's hotel. When Jane opened the door, Anita breezed past her, waving the envelope in the air.

"I got them! It wasn't easy, but if there's one thing a D.A. is afraid of, it's bad press. Speaking of which, you haven't talked to any reporters about this, have you? Here in New York or in Washington?"

"Good grief, no!" exclaimed Jane. "I told Claire not to even discuss it too much at home, for fear of influencing her memories."

"Good. Now, here are the photos." She laid them out on the table. "Mike Kingsbury you've met. That's Christina, about four months before her death, at her father's New Years bash. Paul Solderburg himself, this is the housekeeper and the chauffeur, you might not need those, and the private investigator. There were some minor witnesses, bartenders or something, but I have no pictures of them. This is Marlene Endicott; she was Christina's best friend. We were going to call her as a witness, but found out she really didn't know anything; she had moved to Boston, and she and Christina hadn't seen each other for awhile. She still attended the trial, though, every day of it."

"Really?" Jane frowned. "Claire said the person who killed her was someone she knew very well but wasn't close to. I've been thinking "man" all this time, but a woman could have pushed her into that mantle, couldn't she?"

"Wow, that's a new slant." Anita thought a moment. "'Knew well, but wasn't close to,' could mean distance or emotion. That covers a lot. I would say it lets out her father, though. Are these enough?" Anita asked.

"These will do nicely," said Jane, gathering them back into the envelope. "I will return them as soon as I can." She carefully placed the envelope in her briefcase. "Now, I have to go, I'm on standby for a flight this evening. It was great to see you again, Anita, and I hope we can get to the bottom of this."

"Me, too. Have a nice flight." Anita hugged her and left. Jane finished packing and took one last look around, then left her hotel room to head to the airport and home.

Chapter 27

Washington State
Friday, June 20th, 2008
3:00 AM

Red-eye flights are so appropriately named, Jane thought grimly as she waited for her luggage at the carousel. Other bleary-eyed people, who also had flown into SeaTac Airport in the wee hours of the morning, either on purpose or as the result of a missed flight, surrounded her. Spotting her bag, she grabbed it and headed outside to catch the shuttle back to her home. She hoped to catch a few hours of sleep before she called the Warners. Waking at nine a.m., she showered and dressed, then dialed the Warner's number. Reaching only voice mail, she left a message stating that she would like to come out that evening, and to call her office if it was inconvenient. Then she gathered up her paperwork, and started to leave. Stopping in mid stride, she set everything down, and went to the hall closet. She pulled down a box from the shelf and carried it to the table. Pulling out several photographs, she leafed through and found some that were the same size as the ones given to her by Anita. Shuffling them together, she placed the rest of the photos back in the box and returned it to the shelf. Once again, she gathered her things, and this time she left home and drove to her office. Picking up her new schedule from her receptionist, she noted with approval that all her appointments had been moved to at least next week. That gave her the rest of this week to work on this Warner/Kingsbury mystery.

Once in her office, she checked the messages on her personal machine, taking notes and making phone calls. At five, when she hadn't heard from the Warners, she left the office and headed for Enumclaw. Carl and Sandra met her at the door.

"How was your trip? How was your conference? Did you find out anything?" Sandra and Carl excitedly bombarded Jane with questions. Laughing, she held up her hands in mock surrender.

"I can only answer one question at a time," she said, "And before I answer anything, I want to talk to Claire."

"She's in the living room," said Sandra. "We have iced tea there, unless you would like something else. We hope you will stay for dinner?"

"I'd love to, and iced tea is fine. We'll talk to you both in a few minutes."

Jane made her way into the living room, and took off her coat, laying it across a chair. Opening her briefcase, she removed the envelope of pictures and sat beside Claire on the sofa.

"Hello, Claire, how are you feeling?"

"Hello, Dr. Radcliff. I feel fine. I haven't remembered anything important, just flashes of stuff. I wrote it all down." She indicated her journal, which lay on the coffee table.

"That's fine, Claire, we'll read it if we need to. Meanwhile, I want you to look through these pictures and see if you recognize anyone." She handed Claire the photos and sat back to watch her face. Claire began looking through the pictures.

"Daddy." She smiled softly as she saw the picture of Paul Solderburg. She set that one on the coffee table. She named Mike Kingsbury and the one of Marlene Endicott, although she frowned a little at that one. She smiled also at the one of Christina, and commented that it had been taken at "Daddy's party". Whenever she saw one of the photos Jane had added, she would frown and shake her head.

"That detective, I owe him money." she said when she recognized the picture of Peter Wallace. She also identified the housekeeper and the chauffeur. Dr. Radcliff took away her own

142

photos, and asked Claire to identify each of the remaining ones again. Claire sighed, but reached for the photos.

"This is me... Christina...at my father's New Year's Eve party. This is Mike, my husband. This is my father, Paul Solderburg. These are the people who worked for me, Nancy Clapper my housekeeper and..." Suddenly she gasped and dropped all the photos.

"No! she said, scrambling to her feet. "It was you!"

Then she seemed to waver on her feet. Jane jumped and grabbed her, easing her back onto the sofa. Waiting for her to recover, she picked up the pictures, and laid all the ones she had named on the table. This left only Marlene's, the chauffeur's, and the detective's.

"Claire? Christina? What is it?" Jane asked gently when Claire stopped shuddering. Claire focused on Jane's face with difficulty. Then she shook her head as if to clear her thoughts. She reached for the pictures in Jane's hand, and chose one of them.

"Him. Steven, my chauffeur. He is the man who robbed and killed me." Jane took the picture from her, and tilted Claire's face up so she could look into her eyes.

"Are you sure?" she asked gently, "we don't want to accuse anyone without proof."

"I'm sure," Claire said firmly. "He was wearing a black mask – a ski mask – but I managed to rip it off his face. That's why he pushed me."

"Claire, when you were Christina, what was your favorite candy and why?" Claire looked at her with a blank expression. Then she began to speak in a soft voice, as though she were far away.

"My mother had never tasted cherry cordials until my father bought them for her on the first Valentine's Day after they were married. He would buy her a box every year. She would eat one a day to make them last. When I was old enough, she would share them with me. I'm not sure how Mike found out, but the first year we were married, he bought me a box of cherry cordials. I ate one every day to make them last." She smiled, and seemed to come back into the room. "Marlene thought I was crazy until I explained it to her. I offered to share them, but she didn't like them."

"What was your favorite flower?"

"I love flowers. I'm not sure I have a favorite, unless it's white roses, because they remind me of my mother. It's the only flower Daddy ever bought her.

"Are my father and husband still alive?" Claire asked, a glimmer of hope in her eyes.

"Christina's husband is still in prison for her murder," Jane said firmly. "You are going to upset your parents if you continue to refer to Paul Solderburg as your father. He died in 1998."

"You're right, Doctor, I will be more careful," said Claire. Just then, Sandra announced dinner.

When they sat down, Carl asked if everything was alright.

"Well, there is nothing mentally or physically wrong with Claire's brain, nothing you need worry about on that score," Jane reassured him. "As far as these memories she seems to have are concerned, I am still working on that."

"What can we do to help?" asked Carl. "I don't want this upsetting our family any more. If we all stop talking about it, maybe it will stop."

"That's not the way it works," Jane said gently. "If indeed Claire is the reincarnation of Christina, and Christina came back to clear her husband's name, it's possible that she will take over more and more of Claire's mind and memory until someone listens to her. Reincarnation was one of the beliefs I studied very thoroughly before deciding on this line of work. Ignoring it can make a person crazy." Claire could not remain silent any longer.

"I'm not crazy! Why won't you believe me?" Claire exclaimed.

"I'm not saying I don't believe you, Claire. You've never tried to convince me that you are Christina, merely that you have her memories. This could also be clairvoyance, but I've seen no prior evidence of that in your life, either."

"So what do we do now?" Sandra herself was close to tears.

"I'm going to contact another specialist, Dr. Mohan. He was my professor in college, and we became good friends. He is from India, where the belief in reincarnation is traditional and revered. He will know what the next step should be." She turned her attention back to her plate, and by mutual agreement, the subject was dropped for the remainder of the meal.

Sandra sent Claire to bed. Carl and Sandra sat up talking with Dr. Radcliff. They agreed that they had to see this through for Claire's sake. She needed their support now more than ever, and she would have it. No one slept well in the Warner house that night. Claire was worried that the doctor would not be able to find the proof she needed to clear Mike Kingsbury, and put the real killer behind bars. Claire's parents were worried about what this was doing to Claire's life. After all, she was sixteen; she should be going to dances and parties. Instead, she was involved in a murder case from across miles and years. Everyone was praying it would be over soon.

Chapter 28

Jane waited on hold for Dr. Mohan to pick up the phone. When he did, she identified herself, spending a few moments in small talk, a little catching up.

"Doctor, I need your help on an interesting case," she said as soon as she politely could. "Do you have any time free this afternoon?"

"This afternoon?" She heard the rustle of papers as Dr. Mohan checked his schedule. "Yes, I have about an hour free at one-thirty. It must be important."

"There's a possibility that it could mean a man's life," Jane said, anxiously.

"Well, I'll see you at one-thirty, I can't wait to hear about it." They hung up, and Jane decided to organize her notes, so that she wouldn't waste too much of Dr. Mohan's time.

Dr. Mohan, a well-known psychiatrist, looked very much the part, a distinguished gentleman, born and educated in India. It was while teaching at the University of Washington that he gained his international notoriety. He loved the cool climate of Washington State and had taught at the university for the last thirty-two years. His fine high cheek bones and distinguished graying hair lent an air of authority to the knowledgeable, yet unassuming man. He often laughed inwardly when he heard people describe him with terms like, "authority" and "master clinician"; he felt no different than he had as an eager young student in India. When Jane Radcliffe was seated in Dr. Mohan's office, he took off his reading glasses and leaned back in his chair.

"Do you mind?" he asked, motioning to his pipe.

"Of course not, feel free." Jane agreed. The room filled with the sweet aroma of fine tobacco. Jane noticed that, although she had heard the doctor was over sixty-years old, he appeared no more than fifty. He had none of the characteristics of old age, and possessed a lively and engaging manner. She was captivated by his intelligent eyes and caring smile. Like so many, she immediately felt at ease.

"Now then, Jane, suppose you start from the beginning. I had an appointment cancel, and my afternoon is yours." He smiled and gestured for her to speak. Jane took a deep breath. She was not expecting to have time to tell him the whole story; this was a bonus! She began with Dr. Cannon's phone call, and was not interrupted until she got to the part about the photographs.

"She said 'this is me' and she called them 'my husband' and 'my father'?" he asked, obviously surprised.

"Yes, she periodically wavers back and forth between saying 'me' and 'Christina', but the first person is becoming more and more prevalent."

"She did not ask who the people were in the photos you added?" he sounded surprised.

"No, just shook her head as if she was aware that she shouldn't know them." Dr. Mohan was quiet for a moment, mulling over what Jane had just described.

"This is indeed an interesting case. I don't want to give you a lecture on extra-sensory perception, but I have to give you a brief explanation. There are many phenomena in this universe that are not widely accepted by western civilization. However, eastern civilization, where, I will remind you, the majority of the world's population resides, has embraced these phenomena for centuries." He continued, almost as lecturing in one of his University classes.

"Telepathy is a person's awareness of another's thought, without any communication through normal sensory channels. Clairvoyance is knowledge acquired of an object or event without the use of the senses. Precognition is knowledge a person may have of another person's future thoughts, or of future events. Psychokinesis is a person's ability to influence a physical object or an event, by merely thinking about it. And," he stopped briefly to identify the importance of this point in particular, "reincarnation is a person having knowledge of another person's life memories, who has died. With our human limitations, we cannot imagine eternity. We try to define everything by the span of one lifetime. This case sounds more like a reincarnation. Hindus and Buddhists believe in reincarnation. You have to ask yourself, can something that millions and millions believe be void of some factual basis?" He took another long draw on his pipe.

"Well, whatever this is, reincarnation, clairvoyance, sixth sense, extrasensory perception or some other power, we can't ignore it. Claire's well being, as well as that of the man in jail, depend on getting to the bottom of things. Here is what I suggest; take Claire to New York. Confront her with the reality of Christina's life. If she is making all this up for whatever reason, she won't be able to keep it up there. If, however, she is really Christina, everything will be clearer in familiar surroundings, and you may be able to uncover the proof that you need to go to the authorities. You say your friend Anita is already on your side?" he asked, raising his eyebrows in question.

"Yes, but I don't think she has been able to convince the D.A., or she would have called. We have to come up with more than just Claire's word in order to have him re-open the case and investigate this chauffeur, or driver."

"Well, I wish you the best of luck, this is a fascinating case. Be sure and let me know what happens in New York, I almost wish I could go with you." Jane laughed.

"I wish you could, too. I'm sure you could solve this puzzle faster than I can." She stood and shook Dr. Mohan's hand.

"Thank you so much for your time. Just saying it all out loud has been a big help. I'll call you when I get back to Seattle and take you to lunch." she promised.

"I'd like that, Jane, it's been too long." She turned and left his office, feeling much more relieved than she had before.

Sandra opened the front door with a smile.

"Dr. Radcliff, we weren't expecting you! Claire is not home from school yet."

"No, I wanted to talk to the two of you without her. I called your husband at work, he should be here soon." Just then, Carl's truck pulled into the driveway. As he came up the steps, Sandra held the door open so they could both enter. She wore a worried look, but she managed to ask if Jane would like something cold to drink.

"Actually, let's talk in the kitchen. You could make some of that delicious iced tea, and I could explain why I'm here." They agreed, and soon Jane and Carl were seated at the table while Sandra made the tea. "First, let me tell you to stop worrying. We are going to get to the bottom of this, and Claire will eventually be back to her normal self. Even if she is Christina reincarnated, that personality should retreat back into submission once we figure out the puzzle that made it emerge. I didn't believe her at first, but now I'm sure there's something there. Dr. Mohan recommended that I take Claire to New York, and I agree with him." This last was said directly to Sandra, who gasped and stared at Jane. "If Claire is making this up, New York will be too much for her to handle. If she really is Christina, or is receiving some kind of message from her, New York is where the answer lies. Will you let me take her?"

"I don't know... she's never been away from home." Sandra protested.

"One or both of you are welcome to come with me. I just wasn't sure you could take the time off from your company," Jane suggested.

"I have good people working for me," Carl replied. "As long as I am not gone too long, I can get time off. How about you, Sandra?" Sandra carried the pitcher of tea to the table, and returned to the cupboard for glasses. She spoke quietly and thoughtfully.

"I want this to be over. If a trip to New York is what it takes, then the Warners will go to New York." Carl turned back to Jane.

"So far we've been able to keep this out of the papers. If the case is re-opened, won't that create a lot of publicity? I don't want my daughter's life to become a media event." Carl sounded concerned.

"I will do my best to see that Claire's name is kept out of the papers. I'm sure Anita would agree to this, and Larson won't want the world to know he's doing this on the word of a sixteen-year-old. We should go next week. Talk to Claire and see if she has any objections to going. Make sure she can take the time away from school without hurting her grades, as I would sign her out for the whole week. Even if we clear this up faster, you should have some time to enjoy New York." She smiled at both of them and drained her glass. "Now, I will go back and tie up my loose ends. I will have to see some of my patients that I put off last time before I leave this time. I'll let you know when our flight is, and send a shuttle to pick you up." She shook both their hands and left them to talk it over.

The next morning, Jane called to let Sandra and Carl know that their flight would leave at ten a.m. on Monday, and was told that Claire's teachers had approved her time off from school, providing she took some assignments with her, and wrote about her trip. That was a tough one, but she said she would write her impressions of her first trip to the East Coast, and they were satisfied." Sandra said, "I was proud of the way she handled the questions without revealing the true purpose of the trip."

"How does Claire feel about the trip?" Jane asked.

"Half excited and half nervous. She can't wait to see New York, but she's frightened by what she might find there." Jane assured Sandra that everything would be fine, hoping she had told the truth. Jane's next call was to Anita.

"I'm bringing Claire to New York," she stated without preamble.

"Her parents agreed to this?" Anita was skeptical. "How did you manage that?"

"They are coming too," Jane laughed. "You should have seen their faces." Anita reminded her to return the photos, and Jane sobered immediately.

"Those were an incredible help, Anita. Not only did she identify everyone, she fingered the murderer."

"What?!" Anita shouted, drawing stares from everyone around her. Embarrassed, she closed her office door and lowered her voice. "She says she knows who killed Christina?"

"Yes, she freaked when she saw the picture of her chauffeur, and says that he was the one who robbed and killed her. She also answered those questions the same way Mike Kingsbury did. One strange thing, though, she identified Marlene but she frowned when she saw her picture. I thought you said the two of them were close friends?"

"Marlene and Christina were best friends, they'd known each other since they were children. The last time I talked to Marlene, about a year ago, there was nothing but love in her voice, when she talked about Christina. I guess we'll have to ask Claire. When will you be here?"

"We're flying out Monday. Give us time to get settled, maybe we could see you Tuesday?" Anita quickly checked her schedule.

"Nothing going on Tuesday that I can't switch, the day is yours. See you then. I'm looking forward to meeting Claire Christina Kingsbury Warner."

Chapter 29

New York Airport
Monday, June 23rd, 2008
7:00 PM

"That's the last one," Carl declared, placing a suitcase on the luggage cart. "I don't suppose they have a shuttle here?"

"No, in New York they 'cab it' everywhere," Jane laughed. "But we won't all fit in one, so let's see if we can find a couple of them." She led the way to the taxi stand, where they separated. Jane and Claire took one cab, while Claire's parents rode in the following one. As they pulled away from the airport, she turned to Claire.

"Let me know if anything on the way into the city looks familiar," she instructed. She thought she saw Claire's eyes widen a bit, but the girl nodded and agreed.

"Although you don't see as much from the back of a limousine," she said quietly. Claire was also quiet; she appeared to be watching the scenery intently. When they met up at the hotel, Claire seemed a little tired, and they all agreed to call it an early evening. Jane reminded them that they would be meeting with Anita Templeton in the morning, and set a time to meet after breakfast. Claire did not sleep well. What would tomorrow reveal? The next morning, Anita did not want Claire upset by the D.A.'s office, so she came to the hotel.

"I know you've been asked more questions than you thought possible, but I have a few more for you," Anita said after greeting

Claire's parents.

"I understand," said Claire. She swallowed nervously and asked to sit down.

"Actually, I was hoping we could drive around the city. Do you remember where you lived, can you direct me how to get there from here?" Claire hesitated.

"I've never been in this hotel before, but if we start driving, once I see something familiar..."

"That's fine," Anita said. Since she knew the hotel they were in was only ten-years-old, she sensed that Claire had passed another reality check without even knowing it. She led the way to her car, asking Claire to sit in front, and the rest of them sat in the back seat.

"I must ask all of you all to not respond or react to anything I ask Claire, or any answers she gives. She must be allowed to feel comfortable in her surroundings." They all agreed, and Anita pulled away from the hotel. After a few random turns, Claire suddenly sat up straight.

"Do you see something you remember, Claire?" Anita asked her. She pulled over and stopped.

"The Waldorf is gone! The hotel that Daddy threw my thirtieth birthday party at is not there!" She seemed almost in tears. "I can get home from here, though, take a left after the church." Anita drove away from the curb, glancing at Claire as if for directions, but Claire was deep in thought. As the car took a few seemingly aimless turns, Claire suddenly roused herself.

"Stop here!" she said excitedly. Anita pulled up to the curb near a large, stately house.

"What is it, Claire? Do you know this house?"

"Judge Thames lived here. His daughter Marlene was my best friend." She stopped; a puzzled look crossed her face. "She was married to Kevin; they moved to Boston." Anita said nothing, but watched Claire's face closely. Glancing in the rear view mirror, she caught Jane's eye to see if she had heard the name. Jane nodded.

Taking a deep breath, Claire told Anita they could continue.

"Drive three blocks and turn right. Stop just past that large tree." Claire instructed. They pulled up outside the same house Jane had investigated on her first trip. Anita turned around to Jane.

"I took the liberty of contacting the current owners. The lady of the house is willing to let us go in if you would like to." Claire was intently studying the house.

"I would like to go to the back garden, please. It was my favorite place in the world when I lived here." They walked up to the front door and rang the doorbell. Anita explained to the maid who she was, and the lady of the house was called to the door. She was about fifty, with a little gray hair showing, and possessed large, twinkling eyes. She welcomed them all, smiling broadly. After introducing everyone, Anita asked if Claire could take a tour of the house, starting with the back garden.

"Certainly," she agreed. "In fact, if you want to walk around the side of the house, you could come in the back from there." Claire was already on her way before the lady stopped talking. When the rest of them caught up, she was standing in the middle of the garden, taking in deep breaths and smiling.

"Smell that? Those are Mama's rose bushes!" She led the way to the white roses growing just out of sight of the back door. "I used to sit out here for hours, reading and thinking and talking with Daddy or Marlene."

"Let's go inside, now, Claire," Anita said gently. She opened the back door, and motioned for Claire to precede her. After only a slight hesitation, Claire moved into the house.

"Show us around, Christina," Anita said softly into her ear. She didn't want Claire's parents to hear her. Claire nodded, and moved toward a doorway.

"This was the library. The kitchen and dining room are here..." She broke off in confusion.

"What is it?" Anita took her arm "Are you forgetting?"

"No," said Claire. "But there shouldn't be a door here." She pointed at the wall, where there was indeed a door. The owner, coming into the hallway, overheard what Claire had just said and agreed with her at once.

"Yes, that door was put in about five years ago. It wouldn't have been here when any of you lived here." She had obviously misunderstood Anita and thought all of the Warners used to live in the house. Neither Anita nor Jane corrected her. After this, Claire seemed to gain confidence. She named every room in the house, explaining what they used to be. On the way upstairs, she stopped and seemed afraid to go on. After a reassuring squeeze from Jane, she continued up the stairs and stopped in front of a door.

"This is it. This is the room I slept in. This is the room I died in.

"Do I have to go in here?" Claire pleaded, ignoring the gasp from her mother. Sandra started to speak, but Jane stopped her with a look.

"Claire, this will not just go away. There is a reason behind this, and I think we need to face this and put an end to it."

"Alright," Claire said sadly, slowly opening the door. She closed her eyes as she walked into the room. Jane noticed that she found the light switch as though it was her own bedroom back home in Enumclaw. Three steps into the room, Claire slipped off her shoes and walked in her nylons over to the opposite wall before she opened her eyes.

"There was a vanity here," she said. "One here, and one over there," she pointed. "Here was the safe, and there..." She turned and walked over to the fireplace, trembling all over, laid a hand on the mantle. "Here's what I hit when he pushed me." Her voice broke and she hid her face in her hands.

"I've had enough!" Sandra declared. "We are leaving right now!"

"Yes," Jane agreed, "We can leave now." They hurried downstairs, Claire still weeping softly. After thanking the woman who now lived there, and reassuring her that everything was fine, they got back in Anita's car and she drove them back to the hotel. The Warners got out first, and took Claire up to her room to rest.

Anita laid a hand on Jane's arm, indicating that she wanted to talk to her.

"I'm convinced. Now how am I going to convince David?" Anita said.

"Maybe this will help," Jane said, removing a micro-cassette recorder from her coat pocket. "I've had it on since we left the hotel. Just remember that Claire's name is not to be mentioned in the press. I promised her parents that her life would continue to be as normal as possible, once we solved this. The longer we can keep the whole story out of the papers, the better for everyone."

"I know, I'll do my best," Anita promised.

Chapter 30

New York District Attorney's Office

Anita stood in the doorway, lightly tapping on the doorjamb. David looked up with a frown, his face clearing when he saw her.

"Oh, good, I thought for a minute you were someone bringing me another petition," he said, sounding tired.

"Well, I'm here to petition you," Anita said. "Do you remember when I talked to you about the Kingsbury case?" David sighed.

"I thought you had given up on that. You did get the photos back, didn't you?"

"Yes, I was given them back this morning. My friend Jane brought the young lady who thinks she's Christina Kingsbury here to test her. We took her through the Kingsbury house this morning, and I have it all here on tape. She pointed out the missing Waldorf, the house of a friend, her own house. She knew where everything was, and even noticed changes in the house since Christina was killed."

"If I remember correctly, you told me she thinks we have the wrong man in prison?" Larson was still skeptical, but nevertheless, he was listening intently now. Anita opened the file she was carrying, and handed it to David.

"You may not remember, but at the end of your opening remarks, you made sure the jury knew that the last thing Christina saw was the face of her murderer. Well, according to Claire, that face is not this one," she indicated the photo of Mike Kingsbury on top of the pile, "but this one." She let the photo of Kingsbury drop to the desk, revealing a photo of Steven Mallock, the Kingsbury chauffeur.

"Are you trying to say the butler did it?" Larson laughed ironically. "How can you be sure this wasn't cooked up by Kingsbury to get out and finally get his hands on all the money that he thinks should have been his when his wife died?"

"I looked into that. Paul Solderburg got all of Christina's money that wasn't designated to go to her favorite charities and causes. Her husband couldn't inherit, because he was in prison for her murder. Paul Solderburg's will all but liquidated his estate. There are small pensions for his household employees, all the rest went to charity, except for the fund he set up to maintain the family graves. There is no money left for Kingsbury. That also eliminates the possibility that the Warners are in this for money; there's no one to pay them. In fact, they have doctor's bills to pay, since this all started with Claire's accident."

"Still, before I ask that the case be opened on the basis of a reincarnation theory, let's do a little digging on this chauffeur of theirs. But don't go getting the D.A.'s office into hot water, and for goodness' sake, keep this out of the papers," David pleaded with her.

"That's the one thing that everyone agrees on," Anita smiled and turned to leave Larson's office. That hadn't been nearly as tough as she thought.

"Anita!" She turned around. "You forgot to leave me that tape to listen to." Retracing her steps, she laid the tape in his hands, then headed for the file room to check on Mallock.

At four p.m., she once again knocked at David Larson's door.

"Come in," he answered.

"Anything?" he asked, when Anita open the door. He was beginning to show interest in spite of himself.

"Well, all we know about him from the trial is this: He was the one who drove Mrs. Kingsbury to the bank when she closed the account, so he knew the money was in the house; he was the one that drove Mr. Kingsbury to the Hilton, so he knew she would be alone; he knew she had hired an investigator, so he knew the household was about to break up; he knew all the alarm codes, but not the safe combination, and his only alibi for the time of the murder is his invalid mother."

"So, do we know where he is now?" David asked. Anita smiled.

"We do indeed. He owns one of the largest limousine services in the city, bought out from the previous owner approximately six months after the murder; right around the time Mike Kingsbury was being sent to prison. That's not all," she paused dramatically. "We also know that three years before he was hired by Solderburg to act as Christina's chauffeur and handyman, he was arrested in Chicago as the prime suspect in a bank robbery. There wasn't enough evidence, and the case was dropped. Very shortly afterwards, he moved to The Big Apple." She sounded triumphant.

"Well!" Larson was impressed. He could see that Anita was taking this case seriously, and regretted taking her request so lightly earlier.

"But we can't go marching in and accuse him of the murder based on the word of a child. Somehow, we have to get our hands on solid proof, or get him to confess. If he's already beat a grand theft rap, he's no slouch in the brains department. We have to be smarter. I'd rather Claire did not have to meet him face to face if we can avoid it," Anita added. "What's the plan?"

"The first thing is, I'd like to meet and talk to this Mystery Girl Claire. Second, have you ever met Marlene Endicott?"

"I don't really know her well, but I have seen her at the health club, and I know she and Christina were close - are we bringing her into this?"

"I think we should get her together with Claire, see if she thinks Claire is Christina," he suggested.

"I just thought of something. When we were driving around, Claire had us stop at Judge Thames' old place. She said that

Marlene had moved to Boston, is she thinking of someone else?"

"No, they moved. But in 1991, Marlene and her husband were divorced, and Marlene moved back up here. She bought her father's old place, and still lives there. If anyone can spot a phony, it will be Marlene. She and Christina were friends all their lives."

"How do we get them together without tipping either of them off?" Anita wondered. She wasn't sure she liked this plan.

"You say you ran into Marlene, would she know who you are if you called her?"

"Yes, we've spoken several times. She remembered me from the trial the first time I saw her at the club."

"Good, call her and tell her you've run across an old friend of hers, and you'd like the three of you to get together. If she asks who, tell her you want to see her face when she sees her."

"Alright, I think that will work," Anita conceded.

"Meanwhile, I'm going to check out a few things myself." Anita took that as a dismissal and left the office to call Marlene from her own phone, in case Marlene had caller ID. A call from the D.A.'s office would blow the whole plan before it even started. Larson, too, left his office.

Driving to the prison where Kingsbury was serving time, Larson asked for the Warden. David requested to see the phone log of the prisoners, specifically Kingsbury, or anyone with whom he had shared a cell. The only number Kingsbury had called was in Pittsburgh. Calling it, Larson found out it had been disconnected. The Warden told him that it had been Mike's mother's number and that Mike had told him that his mother had died a year ago. Checking on the other numbers, he found them all to be legitimate, and none of them connected with the Warners or with Mallock. David then asked about visitors. He was informed that the only visitors Kingsbury had ever had were the two women that had been there a week ago.

"Oh, and the society dame that has been here a couple times. Kingsbury keeps to himself and doesn't cause any trouble. As long as he gets his girlie magazine regular, he's a happy man," the warden said with a laugh. David thanked him and headed back to his office. Back in his office, David called the District Attorney in Washington State. Explaining who he was, he asked for records on Carl, Sandra, and Claire Warner. He was informed that there was nothing on any of them. Thanking him, he hung up and began hatching out his plan.

Chapter 31

Anita rang the doorbell of the Thames' place. When Marlene opened the door, she seemed puzzled to see Anita accompanied by David Larson.

"I thought this mystery person was a female." She opened the door and motioned them both in.

"This is my boss, David Larson, the District Attorney." Anita introduced him to Marlene.

"Yes, I recognize him," Marlene stated coldly. She shook hands with him and led them into the front room, where they all took a seat.

"What exactly is going on, Anita?" Glancing at David, who nodded at her to speak, Anita turned to Marlene and explained.

"We have a person here in New York who claims to be a friend of yours that you haven't seen for many years. Her identity could be important in a case, and we need you to identify her for us." Marlene looked from one to the other. She considered their request for a minute, seemed to come to a decision and nodded her head.

"What do you need me to do?" David took over at this point.

"Do you have a room with two entrances that we can separate with a screen or some partition, and four chairs?"

"Yes, of course, the dining room would be perfect." Standing up, she motioned for them to accompany her, and led the way into a room on the opposite side of the hallway.

"Normally, there would be a very large table in the middle of this room," she explained, "but it's being refinished. Here are chairs, and we can bring in the Chinese screen from the library.

Michael!" She shouted. A man poked his head through the doorway that lead to the kitchen.

"Bring me the Chinese screen from the library, and put it in here so that it blocks that door from this one." He nodded and disappeared. "Now, I will just slip into the kitchen and see about refreshments while you arrange this little puzzle, shall I?"

"That would be great. I hope you don't mind my saying so, but you almost seem to be enjoying this," Anita noted.

"My dear, I grew up on Perry Mason, the reruns." She winked at them and disappeared into the kitchen. Just then the man came back in through the hall door, carrying a large carved screen. He arranged it to block the two doors from each other.

"Anything else I can do?" They instructed him to place two chairs on either side of the screen, all facing towards it. He did so and then left the room to return to his other duties. Anita marveled at the way Marlene trained her help. The man hadn't even shown the least bit of curiosity. She looked at her watch, then nodded to David. He moved around to the kitchen side of the screen, and Anita walked into the hallway just in time to hear the front doorbell. When the housekeeper opened the door, she told her that the guests were her responsibility, and the woman went back to her chores. Anita greeted Jane and Claire, who were looking around curiously.

"Have you been here before, Claire?" she asked gently.

"A long time ago," Claire said. "Why am I here now?" she looked puzzled.

"Come on in here," Anita said, leading her into the dining room and seating her in one of the chairs. She asked Jane to sit in the other one, then went to the opposite side of the screen. David indicated that he had the recording equipment set up, motioning for Anita to go to the kitchen to retrieve Marlene. She held a finger to her lips so that Marlene knew to speak quietly, and showed her that the conversation was being recorded. Marlene nodded. She took the chair that Anita indicated. Anita cleared her throat.

"Can both of you hear me?" Hearing two answers from the

other side of the screen, she turned to Marlene.

"I want you to ask questions of the friend on the other side of the screen. From your questions and her answers, see if you can tell me who she is." Marlene nodded, her eyes sparkling.

"How long have we known each other?" Marlene began.

"About twenty years," Claire responded nervously.

"Where did we meet?"

"I first saw you at piano lessons, but we were introduced in this house."

"We had piano lessons together?" Marlene sounded surprised.

"No, not together, I was leaving when you were arriving. I was older and in the advanced class."

"What year was that?"

"1978," Claire replied. Marlene frowned.

"But you said...when did I see you last?" Marlene sounded confused.

"1991."

"When I left New York?"

"No, I saw you a few times after you moved. I'm talking about when you left New York and went to Boston."

"Were we neighbors?"

"We lived fairly close, a few blocks. Mostly we were best friends."

"What is your favorite food?" Marlene asked.

"Lasagna, and yours is sushi." Marlene started to laugh, then caught herself.

"Tell me a secret. Something I told you and no one else."

"Well, your father thought your first date was at seventeen, but when you were sixteen, you told him you were coming to my house and went out with a senior. He got fresh with you, and tried to get you into the back seat, and you slapped him and ran to my house. I also know that you had a crush on my husband." Marlene stood up and swayed unsteadily.

"No, it can't be! Christina?" She walked around the screen and stood staring at Claire and Jane.

"You aren't Christina, neither of you, how do you know these things? What is your connection to Christina? Which one of you answered the questions?

"I did." Claire's eyes were full of tears.

"Is this some sort of sick joke?" Marlene demanded, turning on Anita, furious.

"No, it's deadly serious," Anita said calmly. "If we could all go and sit down, I'll do my best to explain it to you." When they were all seated in the living room with coffee and pastries, Anita told Marlene that this was all confidential and that it was important that she agree to not discuss it with anyone. When Marlene nodded, she began her story. Marlene's eyes grew misty when she looked at Claire, having trouble containing her tears as Anita talked.

"I have all of Christina's photo albums," Marlene said once Anita finished the story. "Her father gave them to me right before he died. May I see Claire alone for a few minutes?" Jane looked at Claire to see if she objected, but Claire nodded and said that would be fine. The two of them went into the library and were gone for about fifteen minutes. When they returned, they were laughing like old friends.

"She knows things I never told anyone else. Even the sushi joke." For the others, she explained. "I don't really like sushi. I said that once to impress a boy; he made me eat it. Christina never let me forget." Everyone smiled, but no one wider than Claire and Marlene. David Larson touched Anita's arm, to say, "Well, this is good enough for me. We start on Mallock as soon as possible. Mrs. Endicott, I thank you for your help. If we should need your help again, will you be available?"

"Mallock? Christina's driver, Steven Mallock? What does he have to do with this?" Marlene's smile turned into a puzzled frown.

"That's the most important part, Marlene. Claire has stated that it was not Mike Kingsbury who killed her, but Steven Mallock. We needed you to be able to tell us that this was

Christina before we could move against Mallock after all this time," David explained.

"Well, count me in more than ever! I never did like that driver of hers. He would always leave the window open in the limousine, and Christina was too nice to close it. I know your father hired him as a spy," she said, addressing Claire.

"Anita will call you if we need you. Meanwhile, remember what we told you about keeping this confidential," David said as he stood. Marlene nodded, and walked them all to the door. After their good-byes, she instructed Michael to return the furniture to normal, then retrieved the photo albums from the library to spend the afternoon in her room looking through them and reliving her memories.

Chapter 32

Anita walked into Larson's office, her paperwork in her hand.

"How goes the plan?" she said, with cheerfulness and confidence that she was far from feeling; a closer look would have revealed the worry in her eyes.

"Just waiting on a phone call. We're going to have to hire detectives to work up a schedule on this guy. How long can the Warners stay in New York?" David asked.

"I was just talking to them," Anita admitted. "Carl will have to fly back Sunday afternoon, his business needs him next week. Sandra and Claire can stay for another week or two; she is so far ahead in school her grades won't suffer; I've suggested they do some sightseeing today to try to forget why they are here."

"Good idea. It may take a few days before we can establish a routine on the guy. However we approach him, it has to look accidental." Just then, the phone on his desk rang. Scooping it up, he held a brief conversation, then hung up.

"Ok, that's set. We have someone watching him twenty-four hours until we can latch on to a habit we can use to get to him. Somehow, we have to get a confession out of Steven on tape since we don't have any other evidence." Anita smiled.

"We? Is this the same man who laughed and said I tell a real good story?" She laid the paperwork on his desk and stood in the doorway. "Let me know when 'we' have the next step in place." She winked and left his office before he could think of a comeback.

For the next five days, detectives dogged every step that

Steven Mallock took. They reported that his company deployed a dozen limousines, and twenty drivers. Mallock never drove himself; he went everywhere in one of his company's limousines. On Thursday, Friday, and Saturday night, he frequented a bar near his home. Through discreet questioning, the detectives discovered that he was a regular there on those nights. He always came in alone, but he didn't always leave alone. That was all Larson needed to hear. He called Anita into his office on Wednesday morning.

"How are Claire and Sandra enjoying the Big Apple?" he asked her.

"They are actually having a good time," she assured him. "What's the plan? We aren't actually going to use either of them, are we?"

"No!" David was surprised at the suggestion. "I only have them here as a last resort, we should be able to get him this way. I have an actress ready to go tonight. Here's the way it's going to happen..." As he outlined his plan to her, Anita nodded with approval. Too bad Marlene couldn't help with this, she thought. This would beat Perry Mason hands down!

That evening, the private detective actress Larson had hired went into the same bar where Steven would most likely be the next night. She arrived there using one of Steven Mallock's limos, and flirted outrageously with everyone, including the bartender. At about eleven p.m., a man walked in that seemed to attract her attention, a half-hour later, she called Mallock's Limousine Service and they left together. She had made sure, through her generous tips and provocative smiles that she would be remembered when they saw her again. The same limo driver took her back and dropped her at the old Kingsbury Place, where she dismissed the driver, and walked up to the front door with her 'escort'. As soon as the limo drove away, they climbed into a car parked beside the house, out of sight, and drove off.

The next night, the limousine driver whistled softly as he

pulled through the iron gates of Christina's old mansion. His passenger was waiting on the front porch, looking as beautiful as the house.

"Where to, Ma'am?" He asked as he opened the door for her. She gave the name of a bar, which surprised him. She seemed too classy for a place like that. He shrugged. None of his business, he took them where they wanted to go. When they arrived at her destination, the lady paid the fee, then added a generous tip.

"I'll need a ride home, if you're free at about ten tonight," she said seductively, and laughed. "Of course, I'm hoping I'll have company by then." He touched the brim of his cap.

"I'll be out front at ten sharp, Ma'am." She nodded and entered the bar. The bartender recognized her from the night before, and had her drink ready when she got to the bar.

"Why thank you," she said, with a little flutter of eyelashes. "I'm so flattered you remembered." She smiled coyly at him. Shortly after she arrived, there was a murmur of voices as a man entered the bar. Everyone seemed to know who he was; the cocktail waitress did not even consult him before she had the bartender make his drink. It was, of course, Steven Mallock. He sat in his usual booth and surveyed the room. The lovely lady at the bar did not escape his notice, but before he could decide whether to speak to her or not, she was joined by a man who bought her a drink. After a little conversation, he left her, but was immediately replaced by another man, who also offered her a drink. Steven watched her flirt her way through several encounters until almost nine-thirty p.m., when a man walked in that she seemed interested in. This time, she started the conversation, and at ten p.m., they left the bar. From his booth, Steven could see that they got into one of his limos. He made a mental note to find out who was driving, and more about the woman if possible. Then he noticed a friend of his, and spent the rest of the evening laughing and joking with him.

Meanwhile, the lady and her escort were also laughing and joking in the back of the limousine. The driver pulled back into the driveway at Christina's old house. Once they were stopped, the driver came around to open limo the door.

"Will you be needing a car later, Ma'am?" He asked politely.

"No thank you, but, I will tomorrow night at eight." she winked at the driver and added another large tip on the bill. The driver tipped his cap and drove away as they walked up the front steps. When he pulled out onto the street, the lady addressed her companion, "I think Mallock bit. Let's go report to Larson." Going around to the side of the house, they again climbed into a car and drove out through the gate.

The next morning, Mallock checked the log, and called the driver who had picked the lady up at the bar.

"So tell me about her, where did you take her?" he asked the driver

"Same place I picked her up from." He gave the address, and Steven was jolted. The Christina Kingsbury place, where he used to work! This was getting more and more intriguing. He had kept tabs on the place, and thought an older lady lived there alone. Could this be a daughter, granddaughter, or niece? He was determined to find out, but how? That evening, he was at the bar earlier than usual. Instead of his regular booth, he sat at the bar and chatted with the bartender. All he had to do was mention the stranger, and the conversation took off.

"Hoo, yeah, is she a looker, or what? Friendly as all get-out, and a big tipper. If she wasn't so classy looking, I'd think...but I don't get the impression she's looking for customers, just company. Been in here two nights running, went home with a different guy each night. But not the first one that comes along, you know? Like she's looking for something special."

"Well, let's hope she finds it here, huh?" Mallock winked suggestively. "Keep the people happy, they keep coming back, you know?" Just then the lady walked in the door, and the bartender motioned discreetly to Mallock. He watched as she approached the bar, but took a seat several away from his. Catching her eye, he smiled. She smiled back briefly, but then concentrated on her drink. He waited a few moments, then got up from his seat, and walked over to her.

"You were in here last night, weren't you?" She looked at him and nodded slightly. "And the night before, too?"

"So, you're spying on me, or what?" she laughed.

"No, I noticed you last night because you went home in one of my limos."

"Your limos?" she looked puzzled, "What do you mean?"

"The limousine service you hired to drive you the last few nights. I own it." He tried to keep the smugness out of his voice; he didn't want her to think he was bragging. However, much to his satisfaction, she looked suitably impressed.

"Wow, you own the company. You must be a very wealthy man!" she exclaimed, pretending to be impressed.

"Well, just comfortable," he argued. "But I can afford to buy you a drink, if you'll accept."

"Have a seat," she offered.

"So, where are you from?" Steven asked after the introductions had been made.

"Is it that obvious that I'm not a New Yorker?" She laughed, and took a sip of her drink. "Do I have some kind of accent or something?"

"Most New Yorkers that can afford to pay limo drivers also have their own limos." Steven shrugged. "We mostly drive out-of-towners; I guess I just assumed."

"Well, I'm from Chicago," she admitted. "My aunt asked me to come and watch her house while she is on vacation in Europe, and I've always wanted to see New York, so here I am! A friend who lived here told me about this place, and I like it."

"I used to live in Chicago," Steven said, as he motioned the bartender for another round of drinks. The rest of the conversation was spent comparing all the places they each remembered, and Steven failed to notice that he drank three drinks to every one she had. Once, she excused herself and headed toward the ladies room. Instead, she ducked out into the alley in back of the bar and informed the two detectives waiting there that everything was A-OK, and that they would be at the house by ten-fifteen p.m. later that night. She then returned to Mallock, who had not noticed how long she had been gone, and had consumed another drink in her absence. At ten p.m., she looked at her watch, remembering that she told her driver to pick her up.

"Well, it's time for me to go, my car is waiting," she announced.

"I'll walk you out," Steven announced just as grandly, and they both giggled like children. As they approached the car, the driver held the door open for her.

"Home, James!" she commanded. Laughing hysterically, she climbed into the back seat, and soon after Steven climbed in.

"What are you doing?" she said, trying to sound angry.

"I thought I'd get a ride home," he stated. "After all, I do own the company." She dissolved into giggles again and he joined her, not quite sure what he was laughing at. When they pulled in to the grounds, he looked up at the house, wide-eyed.

"Wow, this is your aunt's house?" He sounded impressed.

"You want to see the inside?" she asked, smiling. She made a move as if to pay the driver, but Steven stopped her.

"Hey, little lady, this one's on the boss." He winked at the driver and told him to wait.

"Yes, sir," the driver smiled knowingly. It was well known in the company how much the boss liked the ladies. If this night went well, there could be a bonus in it for him. He touched the brim of his cap, and climbed back in the car to settle in for awhile.

As they walked up the front steps, Steven made a mental note of the changes that had been made since he worked there, still cautious enough to keep silent about his observations. He didn't want her to know that he had been here before. Steven was so intent on getting inside that he completely missed the van parked alongside the house. Inside, detectives monitored every move he made; they had sent the lady who owned the house on a real vacation to ensure that there was no one in or around the house.

The detectives had placed microphones and cameras in every room. The woman turned to Steven and smiled as she dug in her purse for her key; she was thoroughly enjoying this little drama. Years ago she worked as a records clerk at the DA's office and she had found it boring; this job was risky and fun. She unlocked the front door, and turned off the alarm with the keypad. Turning on the lights, she swung her arm and said,

"Welcome to my humble abode!" She waved her arm, encompassing the room. "Can I fix you a drink? Or would you like a tour?"

"What's wrong with both?" Steven asked. "This is definitely a nice place you've got here." He waited for her to lead the way into the dining room where the bar was located. He noticed the new door, but said nothing. She made his Scotch and soda, then started gave him a guided tour through the house, acting as if she were a tour guide in a museum. When she approached the stairs leading to the second floor, Steven hesitated.

"Maybe I'd better go now," he said, downing the last of his drink. She sauntered up to him and took the glass out of his hand, setting it on the hall table. Then she slid her hands up the front of his jacket.

"What's the matter, don't you like my house? Or is it me?"

"No," he said, trying to ignore the feelings her caresses were causing. "I just...I have to go to work tomorrow."

"Oh pooh, you're the boss. Just go in late, it's Saturday." She started to remove his tie, but he stopped her.

"I thought you liked me," she pouted, her brow creased with a frown.

"I do like you, but why can't we just party down here?" Steven swallowed nervously. He was wishing he could have another drink.

"Because I'm not that kind of girl," she whispered seductively in his ear. "I wouldn't feel right unless we did it in a real bed." She took his hand and started up the stairs. Reluctantly, Steven allowed himself to be led to the very room in which Christina had been murdered. He almost couldn't bring himself to step over the threshold. Why hadn't he told the girl about his former job? Did she even know a woman had been murdered in this room? She was kicking off her shoes and laughing now.

"You just make yourself at home, while I go slip into something a lot more comfortable." She disappeared into what had been Christina's bathroom. Steven could hardly stand it. He went over to the bed, and sat down on the edge, removing his jacket and shoes. He lay down on top of the coverlet gingerly, failing to relax. It was far too quiet, he wished she would turn on some music, or at least make some noise in the bathroom. The detectives in the van watched as his eyes darted around the room in fear. They looked at each other and nodded. Suddenly, there was a bright flash outside the window then the house shook as the thunder boomed almost simultaneously. All the lights in the room went out. As the thunder died down, Steven sat up on the bed. He thought he had heard a woman moan as if in pain. He started to call out to the woman in the bathroom, and then another flash lit up the room. He was not alone. Near the fireplace, a figure lay on the carpet. With the next flash, he saw that it was a woman, and that she was getting to her feet.

"Who's there?" he asked loudly, trying to sound unafraid. The next flash lit up the room, and it was all he could do to keep from screaming. The right side of the woman's face was covered in blood. She looked just like Christina Kingsbury. She was even wearing the same nightgown Christina had died in.

"Who are you?" he demanded.

"You know who I am, Steven," she said in a hollow voice. "You robbed and killed me in this very room." Steven was shaking uncontrollably now.

"I didn't mean it," he sobbed. "I never meant to hurt you. I just wanted the money. If you hadn't taken off my mask...I had to push you away. I didn't mean for you to die!" he said desperately.

"No, then why did you plan to rob me at night, when I would be alone? Why, Steven, why did you take the money? My father paid you well." She was coming closer to the bed, and pointing at him. "You took all my money and my jewelry. Why?"

"You had that big fight with your husband, and I was afraid you would be moving back with your father. You took all that money from the bank; you would have put it in a different bank soon." He was almost begging her to believe him, now. "You had already threatened to fire me. I was afraid that when your father found out about that, he would have replaced me. I needed the money to take care of my mother. I didn't know she would die so quickly once I put her in the home, I thought I would be taking care of her a long time. You had plenty; I just wanted some. But when you fell, I panicked and took everything." Just then, the lightning and thunder stopped, leaving nothing but an eerie silence. Steven tried to turn on the lamp but it wouldn't come on. He strained his eyes and ears for any sign of the woman he thought was Christina, but there was nothing. Just as suddenly, the room lights came on again, and the woman from the bar came out of the bathroom with a flimsy little negligee on.

"There, that's better," she stated, as if nothing had happened. Steven had had enough. He leapt off the bed and grabbed his jacket and shoes. Ignoring her questioning look, he ran down the stairs. Pausing only to slip his shoes on, he ran out the door and into the waiting limo. Back in the bedroom, the actors in the drama were congratulating each other on a job well done. With this tape, they could get a warrant to search Mallock's house and business, and possibly discover enough hard evidence to lock him up and free Mike Kingsbury.

"Any word yet? Anita asked anxiously, poking her head around the doorjamb of David Larson's office. David looked up and shook his head. "How long does it take a judge to fill out a search warrant? Is he writing it in Latin?" She asked, sounding annoyed. Just then the phone on Larson's desk rang.

"Hello, Larson here," David said, snatching the phone up. "Yes, sir. Thank you, sir, we will." He hung up and said to Anita,

"We got it, let's go." Grabbing his coat, he left the office, Anita behind him, stopping only briefly for Anita to gather up her purse and coat. The search team was already waiting for them downstairs.

"Now remember, this warrant works even if he's not home. Search every corner, but be careful not to do any damage." That understood, they set out for Mallock's place. After knocking on the door, and determining that no one was home, they forcibly entered the house. The team searched every nook and cranny of the house, and was about to give up when there was a shout from the garage. On a high shelf, in the back behind some tools, they had found a small bundle containing a black shirt, black pants, and most importantly, a ski mask and a pair of black gloves. Wrapping the entire box in plastic, they left the house and headed for Mallock's office. His secretary was apologetic, explaining that they had missed Mr. Mallock by just minutes, and asked them if they would like to make an appointment.

"That won't be necessary," Larson explained, showing her his I.D. and the search warrant. She reached for the phone, but he stopped her.

"That won't be necessary, either," he stated firmly. He and Anita stayed by her desk to keep her from notifying Mallock that they were here while the search team went to work. The office revealed nothing either, until they got to the safe. After threatening the secretary with an Obstruction of Justice charge, they got her to give them the combination, and opened it up. There, still in the store boxes, were a pearl necklace, diamond necklace and earrings, and a few other pieces of jewelry that Larson was able to identify from the list Solderburg had given him. They confiscated all of it, and the team took the evidence to Forensics while David and Anita waited for Mallock to return from lunch; one officer remained with them, in case he put up a struggle. When Mallock walked into the office, his secretary stood up and started to speak. Larson put up his hand, and she quickly closed her mouth. David then turned to Mallock and began:

"Steven Mallock", David began, "we are placing you under arrest for suspicion of murder. You have the right to remain silent..." As he read Mallock his rights, and the officer handcuffed him, Mallock grew pale. How in the world had they found him out? They took him down to the police station and allowed him to call a lawyer. When they were seated in an interrogation room, Larson turned on a video player. Silently, they watched the tape that had been made the previous night in the Kingsburys' former residence.

"We have the jewelry from your office safe, and the clothes you wore that night. There was blood on one of the gloves, and it matches Christina Kingsbury's. Why don't you make things easier for everyone and just confess?"

The door opened, a man poked his head through and nodded once at Larson, then withdrew. Larson turned to Mallock's lawyer.

"That was confirmation that the fibers found on Christina's hand belong to the ski mask we found in your client's garage. It will put him away for life." Steven bowed his head, quiet for a moment, then realizing that there was no way out, he started his confession.

"I really never meant to hurt her. Sure, I resented the fact that she had money, and I never felt that I was paid enough. But the only reason I did it was that I thought I was about to lose my job. She got so angry when I let it slip to her husband about the detective that I figured as soon as her father heard the whole story, I was finished." He took a deep, shaky breath. "When she closed the account and brought all the money back, I thought I could just crack the safe while she was out the next day. But the more I thought about all that money just lying there... I knew the alarm code; I gave Mama some extra painkillers to knock her out and went back to the house. Everything would have been fine if she had just opened the safe. But she tried to run. Then she managed to grab my mask. I shoved her away to fix it, that's when she fell and hit her head. It really was an accident, in a way." He looked up at Larson, who fixed him with a grim stare. "I killed her. I didn't mean to, but I did. I got away with it for sixteen years, but I should have known I couldn't get away with it forever. Just put me in prison!" With that, he broke down, sobbing quietly. His lawyer put everything away in his briefcase, and stood to leave.

"Nice work," he said, shaking Larson's hand. "How in the world did you ever suspect him? I thought you had already put someone away for this."

"New evidence," Larson said briefly. "I'd rather not say any more than that." Mallock was led away, and processed for sentencing.

Later that day, David and Anita entered the prison that housed Mike Kingsbury. They were led into a room where he sat without handcuffs. He looked slightly confused.

"Hello, lady lawyer, we meet again," he said when he saw Anita. "Have you finally come to take me out of here?" Larson spoke up before Anita could answer.

"As a matter of fact, Kingsbury, we have. The D.A.'s office owes you an official apology, and I feel that I owe you a personal one. I allowed Solderburg to influence me, and succumbed to the pressure of the office instead of exploring all the possibilities." Kingsbury was silent. He looked from one face to the other as if waiting for one of them to tell him they were joking.

"For real? I'm really out of here?" he said in disbelief.

"You certainly are," Anita promised. "We've already processed the paperwork, and you are leaving with us." He smiled and shook Larson's hand. He started to shake Anita's hand, then gave her a hug and a kiss on the cheek. The three of them left the prison and they drove Kingsbury to a motel in town, where he would be staying until he found a more permanent place.

Chapter 33

"Well, Claire, how do you feel?" Jane was sitting on the sofa in their hotel suite. Sandra had just been on the phone with Carl, explaining to him all that had happened, and telling him they would be home in a couple of days. Claire turned from the window, where she had been watching the traffic.

"I feel like a whole person now," she sighed happily. "I would like to see Marlene again, to thank her for her help." Claire turned to her mother.

"You would like Marlene, I think."

"I know that I like having my daughter back again," Sandra said with a smile. There was a knock at the door, and Sandra crossed the room to open it. Outside, stood David Larson. Stepping into the room, he looked around for Claire. Spotting her, he grinned broadly and took her hand.

"I just wanted to thank you personally for the help you've been in this. Not everyone would have been willing to get involved."

"I was happy to help," Claire smiled. "After all, an innocent man was in prison."

"Until this, I never put much stock in the reincarnation theory," he said wryly. "Now I'll have to re-think a few things. Not the least of which is how to run the D.A.'s office without pressure from powerful businessmen." He then shook hands with everyone and said he had to be going. For the women, the rest of the afternoon was spent pleasantly, shopping and planning the trip home.

Mike sat on the bed, wondering what to do with his day. For that matter, what he was going to do for the rest of his life. He knew he had to find a place to live, and re-establish all his contacts. He wondered what had happened to his business. Then he remembered Marlene. She had come to see him a lot in prison, and written to him, too. She would know who was still around. Picking up the phone, he dialed information and got her number. When he heard her voice on the other end of the line, he was speechless.

"Hello?" she repeated, "Is anyone there? I'm going to hang up."

"No! Marlene, it's Mike. Mike Kingsbury. Don't hang up, please," he pleaded.

"Mike? Oh, my God, is it really you? Where are you?" she said, ecstatic.

"I'm at a motel in town. I've been released. They found the man who really killed Christina. Can we get together so I can tell you about it?"

"Oh, Mike, I'm having a party tonight, and I have a million things to do. Come to the party, it's at six tonight. I'm living in my father's old house."

"Marlene, I'd rather see you alone first, if that's possible."

"Mike, it just isn't, I'm sorry. But we can slip away from the party for a chat once it gets going. Please come." He finally agreed. That hadn't taken him long, now she could finish up her plan. She picked up the phone again and dialed the hotel where Jane Radcliff and the Warners were staying. When Sandra answered, she identified herself and invited the three of them to "dinner" at her house, a small going away party, she said. They agreed to be there at six that evening. This was all working out perfectly. The next call she made was to Anita Templeton. She and David agreed to come over to celebrate the solving of the Kingsbury murder.

When Mike arrived at the party, Marlene introduced him to Sandra and Claire Warner, and Jane Radcliff, without explaining who they were or why they were here. Shortly after he arrived, Anita and David were at the door. Mike glanced at Marlene, questioningly. Marlene sent all the guests into the living room, but pulled Mike to the side.

"Mike, I have to tell you something. I was not completely surprised to get your call. I knew you had been released. Come with me, I'm about to explain it to everyone." She took his hand and pulled him into the room where everyone was sitting, murmuring; when they realized Mike was with her, they all fell silent. Marlene motioned for Mike to sit, while she stood in the center of the room.

"I'd like everyone's attention, please." David and Anita glanced at each other, then at Marlene. Claire separated herself from her mother and stood in the corner by the window, focusing her attention on Marlene, ignoring the puzzled look Jane gave her.

"I have a story to tell you. This story may make you angry with me, it will certainly surprise you and may even mystify you. Each of you knows a piece of the story, and once you hear the rest, I'm hoping that you will forgive me. I was not completely honest with any of you when I invited you here tonight. Before I go any further, I must have everyone's word that what I'm about to tell you will not leave this room. Is everyone agreed to that?" She looked around the room, meeting each person's eyes as they nodded their heads.

"What is the CONNECTION between Claire and Christina? That is the question that I'm sure you are all asking yourselves." Marlene smiled at the puzzled looks on the faces surrounding her.

"First of all, I want to tell you why I worked so hard to free Mike, and how it all happened." She looked over at Mike, adoration clearly written in her eyes.

"The first time I saw you with Christina, I said to myself, why can't I find someone like that? I'm sure Christina knew how I felt, but I would never let myself show you. You were hers, and I had Kevin..." She trailed off and took a deep breath. Then she composed herself. "I'm sorry, Mike. I actually believed at one

181

time that you were capable of killing Christina. The evidence at the trial was so convincing, and you seemed to have such a strong motive. But when I went to see you in prison, I asked you if you had killed her, and you denied it without hesitation." She moved to sit down, and every eye in the room followed her. "Two years after you went to prison, I went through a divorce. I moved back here to New York, and found that all my friends had gone on with their own lives, and I no longer belonged. I was lonely, and I had a lot of time at night to think. I started thinking about how different everything would have been if we could only be together. Then I realized that if you were no longer married to Christina, you could be mine if only you weren't in prison. So, I went back to visit you again. You kept talking about who could have done it, and all the possibilities. You worked out why this person or that person could have done it, and you kept coming back to Steven as the only one with opportunity. I realized that you couldn't possibly keep that up for so long if you were guilty. Then I started to really listen. He had been present during the fight, knew about the bank, had a motive, everything. I encouraged you to talk; thinking that if I had enough information, I could maybe get you out by proving someone else had done it. At first, that's all I had hoped to do, just cast enough doubt on your conviction that they would look into it. Then I asked you why you went out with Judy while you were married to Christina. You told me that Paul Solderburg treated you like a second class citizen and the pressure of his money was too much to take and you found freedom with Judy. Then you said Judy never visited you in the prison, and you found out that she left New York." She stopped to take a sip of the drink she was holding. Mike looked around at the faces in the room. He was having trouble taking this all in.

"I told the truth that day you brought me Claire," Marlene said to Anita and Jane, who were both staring at her with their mouths open. "I never liked or trusted Steven. He was always sneaking around, always listening. So I checked up on him. Less than a year after they sentenced Mike, he bought out a limousine service completely. He doubled the number of cars and hired a lot of new drivers. He bought a condo, and put his mother into an exclusive rest home. I was sure he had done it all with Christina's money, but I had no proof. The more I listened to you, Mike, the more I fell in love with you. I knew you couldn't have done it, and I hoped that you would forgive me for even thinking that, once I was the one who got you out of prison." Mike smiled at her through the tears in his own eyes. Marlene knew she was forgiven. David could remain silent no longer.

"Why didn't you come to the D.A.'s office?" Marlene laughed bitterly.

"Paul Solderburg. He still had a lot of influence in this town, especially in politics. I knew I would be able to do nothing while he was alive. I'm sorry again, Mike," she turned to him with tears in her eyes. "It almost killed me to have to see you sit in prison that long, but I had no choice. Solderburg would have blocked any re-investigation of his daughter's murder." Bitterness was heavy in her voice. "I knew there were only two people who knew the identity of the killer, and Christina was one of them. You remember, at the trial they said she died looking at the killer. My choices were, talk Steven into confessing, or bring Christina back to life. Well, it had been sixteen years, and Steven hadn't come forward yet, so that possibility was unlikely, so I had to bring Christina back to life. I've always been a believer in reincarnation; Hindus and Buddhists believe in reincarnation, they are almost two-thirds of the world population and I have read stories about people coming back or being reborn. It always seems to happen within days after death, so I started doing some research. This was the perfect plan. If I could somehow convince everyone that Christina had been reincarnated, she could tell them who killed her. That's when others got involved." She moved over and sat next to Sandra Warner, who smiled at her. "With the help of a friend at the library, I had been searching birth records all across the country for the two or three days after Christina's death. I came across the perfect match. Claire Elizabeth Warner, in

Enumclaw, Washington, born at almost the exact time Christina was killed. If reincarnation was a fact, I figured that that would be where she would go, as far away from where she was killed as she could get. A friend of my father's teaches drama at the University of Washington, and he helped me get in touch with Claire's parents. They were reluctant at first, but when I explained that we were trying to free an innocent man, and that I would take all the blame if anything went wrong, they agreed to let Claire help me." Marlene stood to continue her story, leaning against the chair. "I started writing down everything I could remember about Christina. I contacted family members, friends, everyone I could remember. It was easy to pretend that I was just getting back in touch after moving back to New York, and then I would always steer the conversation around to Christina. After all, I was her best friend, it wasn't so strange that I wanted to talk about her." She took a deep breath. "The only obstacle at this point was her father. When Paul died, we went into high gear. Claire then had to become Christina. We simply had to set up a situation in which she could hit her head and make it believable. It was Carl that came up with the puppy idea, after seeing it happen to a child on a farm that he was visiting." Everyone turned to look at Claire in amazement. She smiled and nodded.

"It was all an act." Claire began. "I had a private number to call Marlene, and she began feeding me information about Christina and her life. She sent me photos, videos, house pictures and the whole life story of Christina. Unfortunately, she had only known her since she was ten, so we knew we could not fool Paul Solderburg no matter how much I learned. My drama coach taught me the basics of acting: how to cry on cue, when to answer quickly and when to hesitate, how to school my expression if someone startled me so that I could gather my thoughts. I couldn't tell anyone what was going on. My doctors all had to truly believe I was reincarnated, so that they could convince others," Claire explained.

Marlene resumed the narrative. "It was the domino effect I was counting on. At any point, the entire scheme could be foiled by an unanticipated reaction to Claire's unfolding memory of the past. It was imperative that Claire's family doctor believe her. He had to believe fully so as to sincerely work to convince one specialist, who had to believe enough to convince another. The story had to remain compelling enough for these esteemed specialists to convince Anita, who convinced David Larson. The fact that the current D.A. was the prosecutor at the original trial was just pure luck in timing. But even with this break, it was a Herculean undertaking, nearly impossible."

"But why didn't you tell me? I could have given you a lot more information about Christina!" Mike was sitting forward on his chair now, hanging on every word. His tone, filled with guarded surprise and disbelief, conveyed his roller coaster emotions.

"No, we couldn't take the chance that the D.A.'s office would suspect you of setting the whole thing up. That's why I had to stop visiting you, even though it tore me apart. This way, even if they read every letter I wrote you, there would be no proof that you were involved. It was vital that you respond to questions about Christina candidly without any sign of insincerity. Whenever we were able to bring a specialist into play, your reaction was so carefully studied; it was simply a risk we could not afford. If we failed, and couldn't prove that Steven was the killer, it would look even worse for you if you were involved." Marlene slowly made her way toward a rather displeased Dr. Jane Radcliff. "Perhaps you, more than anyone else, doctor, deserve my sincere apology. Your diligence and tireless efforts on Claire's behalf made this all possible. Without you, truly, none of this would have happened. You were betrayed, however, since the work you so generously offered on Claire's behalf, in truth, went to the benefit of Mike. If it serves as any consolation, your work was not in vain, it paid off in a big way for Mike." Marlene continued, noticing that perhaps Jane appeared a bit less annoyed. "I will of course reimburse all of your expenses, and pay your normal fee plus twenty-five percent. I am sorry that your research in reincarnation ended with such a surprise. Please don't feel bad, billions of people believe in reincarnation. Just because it was not the case here does not mean it can't exist." After a long moment of contemplation, Dr. Radcliff spoke up.

"I must agree that my work ended in success, given the outcome for you and Mike. My groundwork, however, is nothing when compared to the task you have undertaken and accomplished. You are to be commended. Only a woman who is truly in love could overcome such insurmountable obstacles. I admire your faith and courage. It was your unfailing determination that freed an innocent man; the one you love." Moved by the Dr.'s speech, everyone present clapped enthusiastically. Sandra cleared her throat.

"It's true we were paid, but the money is in an account for Claire's college education. We may even be sending her to acting school." Everyone laughed at this, and the tension was broken. They all started firing questions at Marlene, until she raised her hands in surrender and shouted.

"Whoa! One at a time, please! Anita, you first."

"Why didn't you tell me all of this? I would have helped you anyway."

"For the same reason we didn't tell Mike, sort of. I didn't want to jeopardize your job. If it all fell apart, you had to be able to say we had fooled you, and you knew nothing about it. Plus, I felt you stood a better chance of convincing Mr. Larson if you truly believed it yourself," Marlene reasoned.

"Why didn't you speak up during the trial, if you were so convinced Kingsbury was innocent?" David was frowning, not at all happy at the thought that he had been so completely taken in – first by Solderburg's insistence that Kingsbury was guilty, then by the whole reincarnation ploy. "It would have saved everyone a lot of time, especially me. You're darn lucky that you guessed right, as it was. What if Mallock hadn't confessed?"

"Paul Solderburg would never have allowed you to investigate anyone else. He was too big and powerful to fight. Besides, I had absolutely no proof, only my love for Mike." She turned to him, her face lit as if from within. "So, now you're free, Mike. That is, if you want to be." She hesitated.

"Well," he said, getting to his feet. "I don't think I want to be, not entirely. I never realized what true love was. I thought I was in love with Christina, but when I think of what Marlene went through for me, I know that I've never known love before. If this is what Christina felt for me, and I never appreciated it, I feel guiltier about her death than ever. But now that I've been given another chance at life," he pulled Marlene into his arms, "and love, well, I'd like to stay right here and return that love with all my heart."

"No more young blondes? No more playing around?" Marlene teased.

"No, way. I've learned that lesson well." He kissed her, and everyone clapped again. Everyone except Claire. She walked over to them with a calm look on her face.

"Marlene, there's no one I'd rather leave my husband to than my best friend," she said in a voice far older than her sixteen years. They all stared at her, and she broke into a giggle. "I'm going to be an actress yet, you watch." Everyone broke the silence with laughter, and there were hugs all around. David Larson even forgave them all for fooling him.

"If you ever decide to move to New York, I could sure use your talents once in awhile." he said to Claire. Claire agreed to give him a call someday. Marlene announced that refreshments were ready, and the party started in earnest. They celebrated well into the night.